Dedication

This book is dedicated to my lifeline, Jesus Christ. Jesus, I can't imagine going through this life without you in it. Thank you so much for calling me by name and for loving me enough to give your life for me. I will always strive to make you proud. I love you with my whole heart. Thank you for the many blessings you have given me. I love you Jesus...Now, Forever, and Always.

This book is also dedicated to the loves of my life, Danny, Danny II, Brandon, Nicole, Jasper, and Declan. I love you all...Now, Forever, and Always.

© 2021 by Karen Young

All rights reserved. No portion of this book may be reproduced, stored in a retrieval system, or transmitted in any form or by any means – electronic, mechanical, photocopy, recording, scanning, or other without the prior written permission of the publisher.

Unless otherwise indicated, all scripture quotations are taken from the Holy Bible King James Version, public domain.

Faith's Locket

by

Karen Young

Faith's Locket

Prologue

It's a beautiful sunny day here in Bayside, Massachusetts; the smell of the fresh clean air and the sound of the Atlantic Ocean bring a feeling of peace and comfort to my soul. Life is good in this town; the people here are friendly and always ready to lend a helping hand. It feels great to be a part of this community; a neighborhood comprised of families that are willing to make sacrifices in order to meet the needs of others, a body of people that realizes the importance of showing love and respect one to another.

The Braydan family is one such family; they've lived here as long as I can remember. Dr. James Braydan, his wife Nurse Betty, daughter Faith, and Dr. Braydan's mother, lovingly known as Grandma Martha are a very integral part of our community. Dr. Braydan and Nurse Betty work at the local hospital, Bayside Community. They're very well known and loved by many; there isn't a more tenderhearted, compassionate group of people. Their family is the epitome of the patchwork that makes up our community.

The Braydans report daily to their jobs at the hospital with smiles on their faces, eager to serve their fellowman. Faith attends Bayside High and also volunteers at the hospital wherever she's needed. Faith is a senior this year and has many decisions to make regarding her future.

While her plans are to go to college some questions remain. Will she go nearby so that she doesn't have to leave her family, friends, and her volunteer work at the hospital, or will her path take her to another city or state?

Life is full of choices and what we choose takes us on a journey. How will that journey go? Will it be full of joy, sorrow, triumph, or tragedy? When our faith is put to the test will we be defeated, or will we come out victorious?

Chapter 1

It's springtime here in Massachusetts and the students at Bayside High are busy with their classes. Faith's teacher is discussing with her class the significance of names. Why are people given a certain name? Was there a meaning behind it? Is there a great story linked to one's name? Is their name somehow going to influence their future? The questions were thought provoking. The more Ms. Ellie, Faith's teacher talked about this she realized it was not only a great topic to discuss, but it would also be a great exercise for the students to investigate and write about. So, the assignment was given to the students to find out why they were named what they were, and they quickly found themselves on a journey of great discovery.

Faith was eager to get started. She had not thought about her name in depth like that before, but this assignment sparked her interest. On the drive home from school, she could only imagine why her parents named her Faith. Her mind whirled as she wondered about it. Was there a good story connected to her name or did her parents just simply like the name Faith? Before she knew it, she was pulling into her driveway. She parked her car, grabbed her things and went into the house. Time seemed to stand still as she waited patiently, well somewhat patiently for her parents to arrive home. She found herself pacing the floor with excitement, anticipating the conversation she was going to have with them. Every noise she heard outside prompted her to look out the window to investigate and see if they had arrived. When her parents finally did get home that evening, Faith immediately ran to the door and opened it.

"Hi Mom, hi Dad," Faith said, as she greeted them at the door with a big hug and kiss for them both.

"Hi baby girl," they replied in a loving tone. "Is everything okay?" they asked.

Faith proceeded to tell them about the assignment that was given, and she explained to them how excited she was to talk to them so she could find out if there was indeed a great story linked to her name.

"Well, was there a reason you chose Faith?" she heard herself blurt out. "Is there a great story linked to my name? Am I named after some great historical figure? Will my name influence my destiny?"

The questions kept coming as her excitement grew. Dad chuckled as he told her there was a reason why they chose Faith as her name and that they would love to sit down with her and let her know the mystery of how Faith actually came to be. Faith could hardly contain herself; her heart was racing. Dad asked Faith to get them all some sweet tea and then they would meet back in the living room in a few minutes. While Mom and Dad went into their room to get into some comfortable clothes and put their things away Faith went into the kitchen to get the tea ready. As she approached the living room with the tea her parents gathered back in as well. Faith handed her parents their glasses of cold sweet tea and her father took a nice big drink.

"Ahh… there's nothing like being at home with my two favorite girls and a big glass of sweet tea. Thanks for getting it Faith," Dad said.

"You're welcome," Faith replied.

The family settled in and it was now time for Faith to hear the story behind her name.

Dad began by saying… "I don't know if you realized this or not, but your mother and I were married for 10 years before you were born. It wasn't because we didn't want you sooner, but we just had a hard time conceiving. You see, we tried and tried for years to conceive with no luck at all. We couldn't figure out what the problem was. Test after test was run on both of us and there was nothing to show a reason for us not conceiving. Our hearts were broken. We loved each other so much and we wanted a child to share that love with."

"What happened then?" Faith interrupted. "When you found out that there was nothing wrong with you what did you do?"

"Well, there didn't seem like there was anything we could do," replied Mom. She then proceeded to tell Faith that all they knew for sure was that they had to keep trying and hopefully one day it would happen.

Faith again interjected. "Did you always know that if you got pregnant and it was a girl that you would choose the name Faith?"

"No, we had never thought about names," said Dad. "But one Sunday Pastor Dan was preaching and he was speaking on faith and that's where our story began. Let me see if I can tell it correctly…Pastor Dan was reading from the book of (Matthew in the 21st chapter verses 21 and 22 KJV); he basically said that "if we had faith and doubted not that we could say unto the mountain that was in our life to be thou removed and cast into the sea that it would be done." He proceeded to say that "all things, whatever things we asked in prayer and believed we would receive." As he continued speaking, he moved on to (II Corinthians chapter 5 verse 7) and that said, "we walk by faith and not by sight." The next scripture he spoke about was (Hebrews 11 verse 1) and that one said, "faith is the substance of things hoped for, the evidence of things not seen." Needless to say, mom and I were moved to tears. God had spoken to us through Pastor Dan's message; we knew what we had to do. We had to tell the mountain that was blocking our blessing of having a child to get out of our way; we had to believe and not doubt. This thing that was preventing us from having a child we had to have faith that it no longer had the power to stop us. After we believed this we had to walk by faith, not by what we could see with our own eyes, for we now understood that faith required our believing without seeing. It wasn't long after that we found out we were going to have you. When they told us you were a girl we both knew there was only one name that was right for you, and that name is Faith."

"Wow!" said Faith. "That's an awesome story. I've always liked my name but now I like it even more. I can't wait to get started on my paper and by the way, thanks for believing and thanks for naming me Faith."

"You're welcome baby and we're glad that you like your name as much as we do but let's eat dinner before you get started on your paper," said Dad.

"Okay that sounds great," said Faith.

The Braydans walked to the kitchen to get things started for dinner. As they were setting the table and preparing the food their conversation focused on how the day went at the hospital. They spoke about how much they love being able to help those in need and how it makes them feel a sense of worth to be an instrument for God to use in accomplishing healing of others in times of illness and tragedy. Faith agreed with that feeling. She told them that helping others even in a small way is very fulfilling. With her expressing those feelings, Dr. Braydan couldn't help but ask if she was thinking about choosing a career in the medical field.

Faith was still unsure in her decision, but it did bring up the topic of career day. Dr. Braydan was scheduled to be a guest speaker at Faith's school in a couple weeks. He told Faith that he was nervous about speaking in front of the class and he hopes that it doesn't project negatively on the medical field. Faith lovingly encouraged her dad and reassured him that he was going to do great and that she was looking forward to hearing him speak.

"Dad, a lot of the kids are looking forward to hearing you talk about the various careers in healthcare. It's really important for us students to be exposed to the many jobs that are out there. I'm looking forward to hearing the different career talks from all of the scheduled speakers and I pray it helps me make the right choice."

"I'm sure it will," said Mom. "Just take your time, pray about it, and then make the choice that's best for you."

"Okay I will. Wow I can't believe how late it is already," said Faith, as she got up and started to clear the table. "I really need to get started on my paper. Thanks again for letting me know why you named me Faith."

"You're welcome sweetie. Go ahead and get started on your assignment. Dad and I will clean up the dishes."

"Okay thanks guys I'll get started right away. I'm so glad to have such an awesome testimony attached to my name. It's going to make for a great paper. I think I'll work on it in my room and then go to bed when I'm finished, so I'll just say goodnight now. I love you guys."

"Love you too, honey. Good luck on your paper and have a good night's sleep," her parents replied.

Faith could hardly wait to get started. Having the knowledge of how she came to be wasn't only exciting but also inspiring. She thought about how challenges come to everyone in different ways and how one makes it through those challenges reveals their character. Knowing now how her parents persevered in such a trying situation showed her their strong character and revealed to her a great life lesson. Not only was this a great revelation for her, but it was also going to be a great story for others to hear.

Faith went to her room while the Braydans worked on cleaning up the kitchen mess. They couldn't help but smile as they thought about this lovely daughter they had been blessed with. They reminisced about their little girl and how fast time had gone by. The little toddler that once ran around the house was now grown into a wonderful young lady who was about to embark on an exciting new adventure. How was it possible that this child they waited so long for was now grown and ready to graduate? They could hardly grasp the concept. With the kitchen all cleaned the Braydans turned off the light and headed to their room.

As they passed by Faith's room, they could hear her busily typing away on the computer; they looked at each other with a smile on their faces and pride in their eyes. They got to their room, changed into their night clothes, and settled in to watch some TV. Not much time passed and both of them were fast asleep.

Morning came quickly and a new day was upon them. They got up, got dressed, and made their way to the kitchen. It wasn't long after that they could hear Faith stirring around getting ready for school.

As Faith approached the kitchen she said, "Good morning Mom, good morning Dad."

"Good morning honey. How did you sleep?" asks Dad, as he sits at the table sipping on his coffee.

"I slept great thanks; how about you?"

"I slept very well thanks. So, how's the paper coming?"

"Terrific! I've actually finished it."

"Wow! That's great!"

"Yea, I'm so excited to go to school this morning. I really enjoyed writing the paper and we're all going to share our stories with the class. I can't wait to share mine, but I'm also very interested to hear the other students' stories as well."

"Did I hear you say that you've finished your paper?" Mom yells from the pantry, as she gathers things to pack for lunch.

"Yea Mom I finished."

"Great job honey, when will you find out what grade you get?"

"Not until all of the students share their story. Hopefully we'll all have time to present today, but if not, we'll probably finish tomorrow. Well, I better go. Have a great day at work you guys," says Faith, as she gathers her things for school and turns toward the door.

"Honey you really should eat some breakfast first," says Mom, as she comes out of the pantry with her arms full of food.

"I'm not hungry Mom; I'm just too excited about this paper. I'll eat a good lunch I promise. I love you guys."

"Okay, love you too. Good luck with your presentation."

"Thanks," yells Faith, as she swiftly makes her way to the door.

"Wait, will we see you at the hospital today?" Mom shouts out.

"Yes, I'm on the schedule, so I'll see you after school. Love you bye," she yells, as she goes out the door.

"Bye honey," the Braydans yell back.

"Guess we better get going too," says Jim, as he gathers his things. "We have a busy day ahead of us."

"I'm almost ready I just have to finish up here," replies Betty, as she shuts off the coffee pot and grabs their cups and lunches. "Ok I'm all set," she says and the two of them walk out to the car.

On their way to work with the car windows rolled down Betty looks out and can't help but notice how beautiful everything is. The boats are sailing peacefully in the bay, the trees and flowers are blooming in full splendor while producing the most wonderful fragrance. The sun is glistening on the water and the birds are singing the sweetest tune. As she lifts her coffee to her lips and takes a sip, she has a feeling of gratefulness that washes over her.

"What a beautiful day," says Betty. "I can't imagine living anywhere else or working anywhere else. We are so blessed to be able to work at the same hospital and carpool together," she chuckles.

"Yes, that's true. But there's something behind that chuckle, what is it?"

"Well honey it's like this…if we didn't work together, I'd have to drive myself to work. I wouldn't be able to sit here, relax, take in the lovely scenery, all the while drinking my coffee and being chauffeured by you," Betty jokes.

"Ha-ha very nice," says Jim, as he flashes a flirtatious smile her way. "Glad you enjoyed it babe, but the coffee break is over. We're here, time to work. I love you baby," he says, as he leans over and gives Betty a hug. "Now let's go help some people."

"Sounds perfect honey," she replies with a sweet smile on her face.

As the Braydans approach the hospital entrance Dr. Braydan reaches out, grabs the door, and holds it open for Nurse Betty to go in.

"Good morning Dr. Braydan, good morning Nurse Betty," says Hilda and Florence, as the Braydans enter the hospital.

"Good morning Hilda, good morning Florence," reply the Braydans.

"It's a beautiful day out today," said Hilda. "The Lord is truly blessing us with this sunshine and warm weather."

"Yes He is Hilda, there's no denying that," replies Nurse Betty.

"Dr. Braydan, Danny and Brandon from Radiology were looking for you this morning. They have the images that you wanted and said the discs are all ready for you as well. They were leaving them on the desk in your office," said Florence.

"Thanks Florence, I'll review them and see if there are any other images I need. I'm going to stop by my office really quick and check them before I start my rounds." As he starts to walk away, he turns and looks back at Betty and says, "I'll catch up with you soon sweetie."

"Ok," she replies. "Have a good day ladies," says Betty, as she heads to the nurses' station.

"You too," reply Florence and Hilda.

The day was going great and it seemed as if only a short time had passed when from a distance the Braydans heard a voice saying, Mom, Dad wait up. As they turned around, they saw Faith come rushing down the hospital hallway.

"Hey honey, what are you doing here?" asked Mom. "Is everything ok?"

"What do you mean Mom?" replied Faith. "I told you I had to volunteer today after school."

"Is it three o'clock already?" asked Mom, as she glanced at her watch, "my goodness where does the time go?"

"So, how'd the presentation go?" asked Dad.

"It went great! Everyone really liked the story behind my name, and I enjoyed their stories as well. For example, Ms. Ellie, well her real name is Eljelean; she was named after her great grandmother who was a preacher. I think it's interesting how her grandmother was a teacher of God's Word and now Ms. Ellie ended up being a teacher."

"That is really interesting," said Mom.

They stood there for a few minutes longer discussing some of the other stories before Faith revealed that she received an A+ on her paper. The Braydans were very proud of Faith so they decided the three of them would go out to dinner in honor of her excellent grade. Plans were set to meet in the lobby in a few hours when they all completed their shifts. But with work still needing to be done, they hugged each other and then went on their way to help where they were needed.

Faith's Locket

Chapter 2

The end of the school year was quickly approaching. The students have been discussing what their plans are for the future. Who's going to college? What college will they go to? What career will they choose? As you find in most high schools there are some students who know the path they will take after they graduate and then there are others who are unsure. Career Day is usually a big help in assisting them with making wise decisions for their future career goals. Hearing about jobs firsthand from professionals in a particular field can be very enlightening. Dr.

Braydan and other professionals are scheduled to speak to the students in Faith's class. Hopefully when they listen to these respected speakers it will encourage them and help them believe that they can accomplish any goals they set for themselves. It takes hard work and determination, but one can be and accomplish anything if one wants it badly enough.

Ms. Ellie stood up when Dr. Braydan arrived at the class. She reached out, shook his hand, and proceeded to introduce him. "Class I'd like to introduce our next speaker. He works at Bayside

Community Hospital, please join me in a round of applause for Dr. Braydan."

"Thank you very much Ms. Ellie and students," said Dr. Braydan. "It's a great honor and privilege to be here today and speak to you about my career. I really don't want to focus my talk strictly on becoming a doctor such as I have chosen for my career path, but I would like to recommend that you would all in some way consider working in the medical field. There are so many areas of health care to choose from and they're all very important. It doesn't matter if you're the doctor, nurse, rad tech, food service person, or if you're on the janitorial staff. We're all on the same team, working together to help restore health to the sick and afflicted.

"There is a great sense of worth that you receive when you put others' needs before your own. No act of kindness is perceived as small. Not everyone has the ability to perform surgery or the ability to distribute medication, but everyone has the ability to show compassion to others. Anyone can smile, or listen to someone, or give them a shoulder to cry upon. We are all human and it's our job to be humane to each and every person who's in need.

"It's important for you to go to college so you can get the needed degrees that will help you in becoming a competent, ready, understanding, and compassionate servant. I use the word servant because that's what we are when we help others. This isn't a demeaning title it's more a title of honor. Jesus was a servant. He came to help us and show us the way of compassion and if the title of servant is good enough for Him then it should be good enough for us. I'm glad that I choose to serve, and I hope that you will too.

"We need many people in the field of medicine who aren't afraid to serve. A lot of people think it's all about making big money, but it isn't. The pay is good but the feeling you get in your soul when you've given hope to someone who's in despair is worth far more than any amount of money. I suggest that you all take these next few months before you graduate, to volunteer at our local hospital so you can see for yourself what I'm talking about. I could stand here and give in depth description of what I do each and every day, but my job is just one of many at a hospital. Volunteering lets you see first-hand the many different positions available there. Hands-on experiences are also so much more beneficial for you than just hearing or reading about a certain job. Besides volunteering you can also set up sessions of job shadowing with professionals throughout the hospital, which means you can follow along with them as they go through their workday. Experiences like that, actually witnessing someone's job, will help you decide if the medical field will be the right choice for you.

"I'll leave a volunteer sign-up sheet with your teacher and once you've all had the opportunity to sign up, Faith can bring it home to me and I'll deliver it to the hospital volunteer office. The volunteer staff will then contact you regarding hours that are available for you to come in. As most of you probably already know Faith has been an active volunteer for years and I think she has really enjoyed donating her time to help others. I know for sure that the patients have been blessed by her being there offering them help in any way possible. Her mother and I hope that she will seriously consider a career in the medical field. There is such a great need for medical personnel. I hope you will all take the opportunity to volunteer and then make the decision to join in the effort to make this a healthier and happier world, starting here in our own town of Bayside.

"Thank you for inviting me to speak to you today. I hope this presentation has encouraged you to pursue a career in the medical realm. If you have any specific questions regarding what I do or the classes I had to take, or what college I went to, you can write them down and Faith can bring them home to me. I will do my best to answer your questions clearly and completely and get them back to you. Thank you."

"Thank you so much Dr. Braydan," said Ms. Ellie. "We appreciate you taking time out of your busy schedule to share this information with us."

"You're very welcome. It has been my pleasure," said Dr. Braydan, as he shook Ms. Ellie's hand. "I must get to the hospital now. I hope you all have a great day. Bye class," said Dr. Braydan, as he left the room.

"Bye Dr. Braydan," the class replied, as they clapped loudly.

Ms. Ellie turned toward the class and said, "Wasn't that wonderful how Dr. Braydan emphasized the importance of the many areas of employment in the medical field. He didn't place his position above anyone else's. I'm glad he made that point clear. Every job is important! No matter what job you choose it's important for you to do your very best in all aspects of that job. I want you to remember that as you consider all of the different careers that are presented.

"As the presentations are taking place imagine yourself in the position spoken of. Ask yourself questions like: Does this sound interesting enough to me to pursue a career in this area? How many years of college are required to obtain this position? Am I willing to devote the time and money into going after and achieving this goal? And probably the most important question to consider is does this job fit my strengths and personality? Can you see yourself doing this job for the next 30 years or so? Enjoying one's career makes that career easy. When you look forward to going to work it doesn't feel like work at all. Try and pick wisely so you can get paid for doing something that brings you joy and also gives you a sense of value and accomplishment.

"Class is just about over for today so take this time to jot down any questions you might have for Dr. Braydan and don't forget to sign up for volunteering if you're interested. I'll put the volunteer sign-up sheet right here. If you have questions, make sure to give them to Faith so she can take them home. Go ahead and talk but keep it down so we don't disturb the other classrooms nearby."

As the students moved around to talk with each other a girl approached Faith and asked, "Can I talk to you for a second?"

"Sure Marcie what's up?" replied Faith.

"I just wanted to say thanks for getting your dad to come in and speak with us today. He's so nice and the way he spoke about all the careers being equally important really made me feel like that's the kind of environment I want to work in. I want to be a part of a team working for the good of all involved. Law is my passion and I've always wondered what type of law I should get into, but after hearing your dad talk so passionately about being a servant and putting the needs of others before your own, I really feel like pursuing a career in medical law. Working in a hospital setting might just be the place for me. Please let your dad know I appreciated him taking time out of his busy schedule to come and speak with us and I'm definitely signing up on the volunteer sheet."

"Oh Marcie, thanks for telling me this. I'll for sure tell my dad what you said and thanks for volunteering; it's a much-needed service and it's so rewarding. I love it and I look forward to working with you as a volunteer," replied Faith.

"It really is rewarding," Denise chimed in. "I've been volunteering there right alongside Faith for a couple years now."

"That's cool," said Marcie. "I can't wait to work with both of you."

"It'll be fun," said Faith. "And wouldn't it be great if we all ended up working at Bayside Community for our entire careers?"

"That would be awesome," replied Denise and Marcie.

"I hope I'll be able to continue my volunteer work while I attend college," said Faith.

"That would be nice. Where do you want to attend?" Marcie asked.

"Faith and I have both applied to Massachusetts State," said Denise.

"Really, me too!" exclaimed Marcie.

"That's incredible! If we all get into Mass State, we should be able to continue our volunteer work at Bayside Community and then hopefully get hired there when we get our degrees," said Faith.

"Sounds like a plan. Let's get Marcie signed up for volunteering and let's pray we all get accepted," said Denise.

"Ok let's do it," replied Faith.

As the dismissal bell was ringing Marcie wrote her name on the list. With a smile on her face, she handed it to Faith. "Check this out; your dad must have gotten through to a lot of students. Look at all the names on this list."

"This is awesome," said Faith, as she looked at the list. "I can't wait to show my dad. He's going to be so excited!"

The girls started to pack up their things so they could leave.

Denise blurted out, "Hey I have an idea. Do you guys want to go out and grab a bite to eat and talk more about our future plans? Then after we finish eating, we can stop by the hospital and tell Dr. Braydan he did a great job. While we're there we can show Marcie around since she's going to be joining us in the volunteer department."

The girls agreed that it was a great idea. They talked for a moment longer about where they should go eat. They decided to go to The Oven because it's a nice family restaurant not far away and they have delicious food with a great variety to choose from. The plan was set and whoever arrives first is supposed to get a table.

Faith and Denise finished gathering their things and then headed to the school parking lot. Meanwhile, Marcie had already gone to her car and took off toward The Oven. The girls were excited thinking about what the future had in store for them. As Faith and Denise drove up, they noticed Marcie's car, so they knew that she had beaten them there. When they walked into the restaurant, they glanced around looking for Marcie.

"Faith, Denise, over here," yelled Marcie, as she waved her hands up to flag them down.

"Hey Marcie, good table, I love setting next to the window. The view of the Bay is just so lovely; the water, the boats, the sunsets," said Faith.

"Don't forget the view of the guys on the beach," said Denise, as they all start laughing.

"I know, right!" replied Marcie. "Why would we ever want to leave Bayside; the view alone is worth staying for," she chuckled.

It didn't take long before Lisa approached the table to take the girls' order. Faith had decided on chicken strips, spaghetti for Denise, and Marcie chose a burger.

"It'll be right up," Lisa said, as she walked away to place the order.

"So, you guys know that I want to go into law," said Marcie, "but what do you want to go into?"

"I'm thinking strongly about nursing," answered Denise.

"That would be perfect! Nurses are in high demand and I'm sure it must be so rewarding," said Marcie.

"Oh, it is," Faith chimed in. "My mother loves her job! She has told us time and time again that she could never imagine herself in any other career."

"It's great, she loves it so much. I'm sure the patients can feel positive energy coming from her and it must put them at ease having a joyful nurse instead of a crabby one," said Marcie.

"I bet that's true. I've never really thought about it that way." replied Faith.

"What about you Faith, what do you want to go into?" asked Marcie.

"I'm thinking about Physical Therapy," she replied. "I've always had a desire to work in the medical field probably because my parents are in that field, but I really don't want to do the same thing that they've done. I think volunteering at the hospital has made me want to go into it even more than before I had volunteered. Helping the patients and getting them to smile just by showing them you care about them; well, it just makes you feel good. But don't get me wrong it's not always pleasant. Not all the patients are easy to get along with and they may not want your help, but you still have to treat them all with kindness and respect. I think in the long run the majority of them appreciate everything you do for them though."

"I'm sure they do," said Marcie, "but what is it that makes you want to go into Physical Therapy?" she asked.

Without interrupting the girl's conversation Lisa placed their food in front of them, refilled their drinks and walked away.

"Well, I guess it's because I can work with a large variety of patients. It isn't a job that deals with helping the patient get well from like an illness so to speak but more about restoring mobility, helping them to be able to do things. I can help any age patient as a Physical Therapist, and I like that. I don't want to be locked into pediatrics or somewhere in the middle or in geriatrics; I want to help patients of all ages in many different ways and Physical Therapy will give me that opportunity. I might have to move their bodies for them at first but then I'll be able to witness God's goodness as I see them make progress and move on their own. I'll get to be there motivating them and cheering them on and sometimes it will just feel like I'm playing games with them. I think it will be so much fun that it won't feel like work for me. I love helping people and this career is just calling out to me."

"That sounds great," replied Marcie.

"Yea, Faith will be awesome at Physical Therapy. You can tell she has the heart for it," said Denise. "And the patients will love having her as their therapist."

"Awe, thanks Denise, that's sweet of you to say and your patients will love having you as their nurse too. I know that you will be great with them."

"Thanks Faith, I appreciate that. Now we just have to make sure we all get into Mass State and into our programs."

"Oh, we'll get in," said Marcie. "We have to! I can see it all so clearly. First, graduate High School. Next, get into Massachusetts State. Then, work together at Bayside Community. After a few decades or so, we can retire and enjoy old age together."

"Good plan," said Faith and Denise laughing. "We are in!"

"Ok, now that we have that settled and our bellies are full, do we want to go to the hospital, drop off the list to Dr. Braydan and then get my tour of the hospital started?" asked Marcie.

"Sure do," replied Faith. "We will meet you there."

"Ok let's do this," said Denise.

The girls got up, gathered their things, paid the bills and headed to the hospital. Faith and Denise rode together and talked about how excited they were that Marcie was going to join them in volunteering. The thought of them all working together at Bayside Community after college had them floating on air. After they arrived at the hospital parking lot Faith and Denise hurried and got out of their car. They excitingly ran up to Marcie's car and with their arms raised in a presentation way they said, "Well this is it Marcie, your first steps toward your future career destination." Joy and laughter was being shared amongst the three girls as they walked into the hospital.

"Hi Faith, hi Denise," the two women at the hospitality desk yelled out.

"Oh, hi Florence, hi Hilda," replied the girls. "I want to introduce you to our friend Marcie, she's going to start volunteering with us here," said Faith.

"That's wonderful," they said, as they reached out to shake her hand. "It's very nice to meet you Marcie."

"Thanks, it's very nice to meet you two as well."

"Oh no," Florence said with a chuckle. "Here comes trouble, double trouble."

The girls turn and look to see what Florence is talking about. They see that two older gentlemen are walking toward them.

"Takes trouble to know trouble," the gentlemen joked back.

"Faith, did I hear you say that we are getting another volunteer?" asked Phillip.

"Sure did," replied Faith. "Phillip, Clem, I'd like you to meet Marcie, we're going to give her a tour of the hospital and I need to stop and see my dad while we're here."

"It's nice to meet you Marcie and don't believe these ladies when they say we're trouble, it's a web of lies," said Phillip and Clem, as they try to hold back their chuckles.

"It's nice to meet you two also and I guess I'll find out soon enough if these ladies are telling tales on you two," Marcie laughed.

"Oh, she's quick; I like her already," replied Hilda, as she glanced back at Florence.

"Ok you guys we'll see you later," said Faith. "We're going to show Marcie around now, bye all."

"Have fun girls," replied Florence.

As the girls walk away Marcie said, "Oh my they're a hoot!"

"Yea, they are," replied Denise. "You'll find there are a lot of really good people who work here, and everyone is so nice. And of course, the three of us will be here, need I say more," she joked.

"Seriously, I mean it can't get any nicer than that," said Faith.

"I know right, replied Marcie. "We are super nice." The girls are laughing as they continue walking through the hospital.

"So, let's see," said Faith, "Here on the first floor is of course the reception area, the gift shop, Volunteer services, Registration, Administration and other offices, testing areas like the Radiology department where they do x-rays, MRI's, CT scans, and then there's the ER, Pre-op, OR, Recovery, Pharmacy, etc. The cafeteria is in the basement. The second floor is where the ICU is at and where the nursery is, ugh the newborns are so cute. The third floor is mostly dedicated to Rehabilitation. The fourth floor is where the Cardiac unit is. The fifth floor is mostly Med Surg. The sixth is dedicated to Oncology and the seventh is basically for Hospice."

"Faith, there goes your dad," Denise interrupts and points in his direction.

"Oh ok, let's catch up to him," replied Faith. The girls start walking faster in order to catch up to Dr. Braydan. As they get closer Faith yells out to get her dad's attention.

Dr. Braydan turns around with a smile on his face. "Hello honey," he says, as he reaches out to hug Faith.

"Dad, we had to come by and show you the volunteer list; a lot of kids signed up."

Reaching to look at the list Dr. Braydan says, "That's great Faith, we sure can use the help around here."

"Yes we can Dad and I'd like you to meet one of the girls that signed up, this is Marcie. Marcie, this is my dad, Dr. Braydan."

"It's nice to meet you, Marcie," says Dr. Braydan, as he reaches out his hand.

As Marcie shakes his hand she replies, "It's nice to meet you too, Dr. Braydan, and I'd like to personally thank you for coming to class and speaking with us. You definitely influenced me into pursuing a career in the medical field."

"That's great! What area do you want to pursue?"

"Well, I already knew I wanted to practice law, but I was unsure of what type of law I wanted to focus my studies on. After you spoke in class, a career in a hospital setting sounded great, so I've decided to go into medical law."

"That's wonderful Marcie, having quality legal representation in a hospital is very important and I'm sure you'll be good at it. Don't get me wrong, it won't be easy but if your heart's in it then that's half the battle."

"Thanks Dr. Braydan, I'm also very excited about starting my volunteer work here. I know that it will be a great experience and working with Faith and Denise will be so much fun."

"Well, let me be the first to welcome you. I'm very happy that you will be joining us here at Bayside Community and I have no doubt that you'll enjoy it."

"Yea, we'll definitely have a lot of fun," Faith chimed in.

"Girls, thank you for bringing this list to me but I really need to get back to my rounds. Marcie, I look forward to seeing you around here at the hospital and thanks for joining our team."

"Thank you, Dr. Braydan," replied Marcie.

Smiling he turns to Denise, "Good to see you as always Denise."

"Good to see you too, Dr. Braydan," she replied.

Reaching toward Faith for a hug, he says, "Honey, thanks so much for coming by and bringing me the list."

"You're very welcome, Dad."

"I'll see you at home in a little while," he said.

"Sounds good Dad, see you later."

As Dr. Braydan turns and walks away the girls head off in the opposite direction so they can continue showing Marcie around. They walked around a bit more and when they noticed the clock on the wall, they couldn't believe how fast the time had gone by. With all of them having other things to complete that evening they decided to call it a night. Marcie thanked the girls again for showing her around. They walked to the parking lot together and then said goodbye.

Chapter 3

As the morning sun peeks through Faith's window she stretches and pushes the blankets to the foot of her bed. She walks over and looks out the window at the bay and breathes in a breath of fresh air. She can't help but think about all of the wonderful opportunities that lie ahead of her. As she gets ready for the day, thoughts of yesterday flood her mind. She thinks of how much fun she had with her friends and how excited she is to have her future plans in place. She can hear her parents are already up and in the kitchen, so she finishes getting ready and goes downstairs to see them.

"Good morning Mom, good morning Dad," Faith says, as she comes strolling into the kitchen.

"Good morning," they reply.

"Did you sleep well?" asks Mom, as she is preparing breakfast.

"I sure did," Faith replies, "how about you guys?"

"We slept great," Dad chimes in.

Once again Dad thanked Faith for bringing the list to the hospital. They sat at the breakfast table and discussed how surprised they were that so many had signed up. Dr. Braydan had done a better job with his speech than he realized. The evidence was on the paper, but it was also in the news that Faith was about to share.

Faith got up, grabbed a glass of orange juice, and then sat back down. With her leg jiggling under the table, she sat and listened as her dad expressed that he was happy that Marcie was planning on joining the volunteer staff. He also expressed how pleased he was that his speech helped Marcie to decide on Medical law.

"I wonder who else will choose a medical career," he said.

Faith smiled as she looked at her dad. With the excitement mounting she couldn't hold it back any longer, with enthusiasm she blurted out that Marcie wasn't the only one who had decided on a career in medicine. She had her Dad's full attention now as he placed the newspaper down on the table and listened attentively as she spoke. She told about how Denise wants to go into nursing and about how she, herself wants to do physical therapy. By this time her Mom had grabbed a cup of coffee and had joined them at the table. The Braydans were hanging on every word that came out of Faith's mouth; they could hardly stay still in their seats. The smiles on their faces lit up the room more than the sunshine did that was streaming through the windows. Holding back the flood of questions and comments was difficult but they didn't want to interrupt Faith while she was speaking.

When she paused her parents stood up, embraced Faith, and expressed to her how proud they were of her, but they had to ask, "Honey are you sure this is what you want?"

Dad continued, "We are thrilled but it's not easy or always pleasant working in the medical field. There are many situations that arise where you have no control on the outcome and it becomes very difficult emotionally."

"I know Dad, don't worry. I've thought a lot about this and being at the hospital so often has only reinforced my choice. I'm very sure and I'm so excited!" exclaimed Faith. "I've known for quite a while and I've been doing my own research, but I didn't want to tell you until I was positive."

"Physical therapy is a great field. We always wanted you to choose a career in the medical field, but we didn't want to push it on you," said Dad.

"I know you guys did and you didn't push it on me at all, and I thank you for that. It's an important decision to make and just knowing that I had you guys in my corner, so to speak, well it made my decision easy. I love you both for always being here for me and supporting me, but there's more thing I need to tell you."

"Okay, what is it?" asked Mom, as they all sat back down.

"I figured out what college I want to go to."

"Which one?" asked Dad.

"I want to go to Massachusetts State; in fact, I have already applied. They have a great program and this way I can continue my volunteer work and I can also stay at home. What do you guys think?"

"What do we think? Nothing would make us happier," they replied.

"Honey, we are so blessed to have you as our daughter and so extremely proud of the decisions you have made. And to not lose you to a campus far away just puts the icing on the cake," said Mom.

"Seriously honey, you have made our day. We would've supported you going to any college of your choice, but to stay here with us and go to Mass State, we couldn't ask for anything more than that," said Dad.

"I'm so glad you guys are as excited as I am. I couldn't wait to tell you and there's more," said Faith.

"More, how could there be more?" asked Mom.

Faith proceeded to tell her parents that Denise and Marcie had also applied to Mass State. She expressed their dreams of doing internships at BC and hopefully living out their careers there. The Braydans shared in Faith's excitement and they expressed their feelings of joy and positivity that the girl's dreams would all come to pass. They told Faith that hard work and dedication pays off.

"God has a plan, and He will see it through," said Dad. "Jeremiah 29:11 says, For I know the plans I have for you, declares the Lord, plans to prosper you and not harm you, plans to give you hope and a future."

"You know," Mom interjected, "it would be a good idea to request prayer at church this weekend for all the graduates. We need to ask God to help them all make the best choices for their lives."

"That's a great idea Betty; we can definitely do that," said Dr. Braydan. "Pastor Dan will be thrilled to hear that you'll be staying here; he wasn't ready to have you leave your position working with the kids at church. It's not easy to find good servants for the Lord. The Bible says the harvest is plentiful, but the laborers are few and unfortunately it is very true and evident in this generation. We are so proud that you have chosen to be a servant of God. God will bless you for your faithfulness."

"Thanks Dad."

"Faith, you'll have to call Grandma Martha and tell her about your plans; she'll be so happy," said Mom.

"I know she will, I'll call her tonight after we get home from work."

With all the talking about Faith's plans the thought of work had just about slipped their minds. The Braydans got up and started to gather their things for the day. Dr. Braydan grabbed his keys and headed for the car. Faith and her mom quickly cleaned up the table and made sure the coffee pot and stove were off.

Within moments they were leaving the house and were on their way to work. Each one of them was lost in thought as they rode in the car. The city looked incredible. The colors appeared to be more vivid and everything seemed to be prettier if that was even possible. The drive to work that day was one of the most pleasant drives the Braydans had ever had. The future was bright for this family. The joy that filled their hearts was almost overwhelming.

All of a sudden their thoughts were interrupted by Dad's voice. "Ok ladies we're here, let's go help some people and spread the good news," said Dad.

When they got out of the car Faith quickly walked ahead of her parents. She grabbed the handle of the hospital door and held it open for her parents to walk in. As the Braydans entered the hospital they were greeted by Florence, Hilda, Phillip and Clem.

"Ok, what's going on with you three today?" asks Florence. "I mean you always look happy and have smiles on your faces, but today there's a little something extra going on; what is it?"

Dr. Braydan turns to Faith and says, "Honey, would you like to explain our joyous faces?"

Faith took a breath and started sharing her news. The four greeters stood there listening to every word with smiles on their faces. She barely got all the news out of her mouth before she was surrounded by Florence, Hilda, Phillip, and Clem; they all gave her a group hug.

"Oh Faith," said Florence, "we are so happy to hear this. You are such a blessing here at the hospital and at church. We all love you and are so proud of you; none of us wanted you to leave for college."

"Our hospital and church need you!" exclaimed Phillip.

"Yes we agree," said Hilda and Clem.

"We have all been praying for you to make the right decision that would not only help you, but that would also help others and we see that you have done just that," said Florence.

"Thank you so much for your prayers," replied Faith. "They definitely helped me because I feel so much peace in my decision."

"Well now we all have the same smile on our faces," said Florence.

"Thanks for sharing this great news with us!" exclaimed Hilda.

"I thought today was great earlier, but it just got even better," said Clem.

"That's exactly how we feel," said Nurse Betty.

"I really hate to be the one to break up this celebration," said Dr. Braydan, "but there are a lot of people waiting for our help."

"Ok Dad, you're right," Faith said, as she gave her parents a hug. "I'll catch up with you guys later."

Everyone departed and went in different directions. Faith headed to the volunteer office and her parents went to check on patients. As she walked toward the volunteer office, she spotted her supervisor Michelle in the hallway; when she approached Michelle, she asked if they could talk for a minute. Michelle nodded and motioned for Faith to come with her and the two of them went to the office.

"So, what can I do for you?" Michelle asked, as the two of them sat down.

Faith began to share her choices, goals, and dreams. Michelle listened intently as Faith spoke. Faith ended with saying, "I also really want to stay here and continue volunteering if that's ok."

"Are you kidding me?" replied Michelle." Of course it's ok. I was dreading this conversation because I was afraid we were going to lose you. This is great news! Wow, Physical Therapy is a terrific field. I think it will be a great fit for you."

"Yea I'm really excited," said Faith, "and my parents are ecstatic!"

"I bet they are," replied Michelle.

Faith continued the conversation by telling Michelle about Denise and Marcie's plans. "If it's ok with you then I guess you'll be stuck with all three of us. We really want to continue volunteering throughout our college studies."

"That's great news!" exclaimed Michelle." Bayside Community is lucky to have you all."

"Thanks for saying that and for allowing me to keep my position here but I better be going there are a lot of people to help," said Faith.

"You're right about that," replied Michelle, as she reached out to give Faith a hug. "I'm really glad to hear this news Faith, thanks for deciding to stay."

Faith smiled as she turned to leave the office. She walked down the hall with an extra burst of energy in her steps. The feeling of excitement filled her soul. The thought of her future and the possibilities it holds was almost unbelievable. She couldn't help but smile as she imagined what her life might have in store for her. She continued along her way with her first stop being on the Rehabilitation floor. As she approached the nurses' desk a group of nurses along with Danny and Brandon from Radiology started to clap their hands.

"Hey you guys," said Faith.

"Hey to you," they responded.

"What's going on?" Faith asked.

"Oh, just celebrating the good news regarding you staying on here and not moving to attend college far away," Danny replied.

"You heard about that already?"

"Yea, it's spreading around here like wildfire," Brandon answered.

"Oh my!" said Faith, as she could feel her face starting to blush.

"We really are happy that you're not leaving," Nurse Nicole chimed in.

"Yes, that's true!" Kay exclaimed. "And I'm so excited to hear that you'll be joining me in Physical Therapy. We need caring, dedicated people like you in this field. You know I'm happy to help you in any way I can, and you can job shadow me any time you want."

"Thank you Kay. I'm sure I'll have a lot of questions for you throughout this whole process. I'm thankful you're willing to help me and let me follow you around, but I still have to get into Mass State and then I'll have to get into the Physical Therapy program."

The group reassured her that she won't have a problem getting into the program. After a few minutes of talking, it was time to start working. Nurse Nicole instructed Faith to start in Room 27 bed 1, so with that direction Faith was on her way.

Faith's Locket

Chapter 4

A new day was dawning when a crack of thunder startled Faith and woke her from a sound sleep. As she looked over at the clock, she noticed that it was almost time to get up and get ready for church, so she reached over and turned off her alarm. Then she rolled over, covered back up, and thought well a couple more minutes in bed won't hurt. When she heard her parents moving around in their room, she changed her mind about staying in bed; she kicked off her blankets and hurried to beat them downstairs. Faith got busy starting the coffee and getting the breakfast supplies ready. As Dr. Braydan walked into the kitchen he could smell the aroma from the coffee pot. What a pleasant scent he thought to himself, as he anticipated the warm, tasty, coffee going across his taste buds and into his stomach.

"Good morning Faith," Dad said, as he walked into the kitchen.
"Good morning Dad."
"The coffee smells great!" he said.
"It really does but I still don't like the flavor."
"It is an acquired taste," he replied.

All of a sudden, they could hear Faith's mom walking down the hallway.

"Good morning Faith," Mom said, as she entered the kitchen. "What a storm, we're having this morning."

"I know, the thunder woke me up, so I decided to get a head start on breakfast. Here's your coffee," said Faith, as she handed a cup to her mother.

"Thanks sweetie I really appreciate that," Mom said, as she sat down at the table and took a sip of coffee.

Faith got some orange juice and sat down with her parents. They asked if she told Grandma Martha about her plans yet. She told them she did, and that Grandma cried so much she thought she was going to dehydrate. They all shared a laugh. Her parents said they understood the feeling; they too had shed quite a few happy tears. Faith also told them that she shared the news with Michelle at work and before she had the chance to tell her other friends/co-workers, the news had already circulated around the hospital. She explained to them how when she walked up to the nurses' desk yesterday that her friends greeted her with clapping.

"Everyone was really happy and excited for me," said Faith.

"That's great," her parents replied.

"So, what's on the menu for breakfast this morning?" Dad asked, as he browsed through the newspaper.

"From the looks of ingredients, I'm guessing Faith is wanting strawberry pancakes this morning," Mom joked.

"I guess you could say that," Faith laughed. "It's so gloomy outside this morning I figured we needed something cheerful and well, strawberry pancakes make me smile."

"I totally agree with Faith!" Dad exclaimed, as he chuckled lightly.

"Alright you two I'll start working on them," Mom said, as she got up, walked over to the counter, and started to mix the batter.

While mom was preparing breakfast, Faith continued talking. She let them know that Grandma was coming to church and she also let them know she told Pastor Dan her plans. She told them that Pastor was very pleased but not surprised that she was staying and that he felt she wouldn't leave. He believes her calling is here in Bayside.

"That's great honey, I believe that too," said Dad.

"Did Pastor Dan mention anything about having special prayer for the graduates?" asked Mom.

"Yes he did," Faith replied. "He said we can do it at service today."

"Oh that's great! It's so important to lift up the graduates in prayer. They definitely need God's guidance to successfully navigate their way through these life changing decisions," said Mom.

"Yes Amen," agreed Dad.

"That's so true; I absolutely need God to guide me on the path that He has planned for me. I don't know what I would do without the Lord. I want Him to lead and guide me always," Faith said.

The sweet smell of strawberry pancakes filled the kitchen as the Braydans settled around the table to enjoy their breakfast. They joined hands, bowed their heads, gave thanks to God for the food that was placed before them, and for the future that was ahead of them. They could hardly wait for service that morning. It was with great enthusiasm that they finished their breakfast, cleaned up the mess, and got ready to leave for church.

The weather was gloomy and void of sunshine, but as they drove down the road it could not dampen the spirit within their hearts. They arrived at the church hardly even noticing the rain they just drove through. Life was bursting with new beginnings and endless possibilities.

As they walked into the church, Denise and Marcie ran up to Faith with such excitement that the force of their hug almost knocked her over. The girls took off to their seats and the Braydans made their way into the sanctuary. Grandma Martha was already inside; when she saw them come in, she got up, hugged them, and then they all sat down.

Service started promptly and the anointing was flowing. Pastor Dan presented a very inspiring message that led into the graduate blessing perfectly. The youth were about to embark on a new journey as they were preparing to leave their high school experience and venture into a new chapter of life known as the college years. Pastor has always taught the value of seeking God and trusting Him to walk with us in all steps of life. He asked for the graduates to please come up and stand across the front of the church. He then asked for the other members to gather up behind the graduates or at least stretch forth their hands toward the graduates as he would pray for them. He proceeded to say, "Lord, we come before you to ask that you bless these young people, your children, as they venture into this next phase of their life. Illuminate their path Lord and enlighten their minds to know your perfect will for their lives. Lead them on the path that will take them to the destination that you have planned. Give them favor to get into the colleges that will help educate them in their career endeavors. Equip these young adults with the knowledge and ability to fulfill the callings you have placed in their lives. Let them become servants like you, as you have so graciously showed us in your word. Help them to become and accomplish all you have created them to be and let them be a blessing to others along the way. Let all the Glory be yours. In Jesus' name we pray. Amen." Pastor proceeded to thank everyone for coming to church and asked the Lord to bless everyone with a wonderful week, then church was dismissed.

Standing up and leaning toward his mother Dr. Braydan said, "Mom, would you like to join us for lunch today?"

"Oh, thank you sweetie, but I already made plans to grab a quick bite with Hannah and Jay before we head over to the nursing home to visit with those that are shut in," replied Grandma Martha.

"Okay Mom, that's fine, you guys have a good time, and we'll talk to you later."

The Braydans hugged Grandma Martha and then they gathered their things so they could leave. Faith, Denise, and Marcie were walking towards them. When the girls got closer Faith asked if there were any plans for lunch. Dr. Braydan said he wanted to go to Outback, and he asked Denise and Marcie to join them. The girls excitedly accepted his offer. Faith asked if she could ride with her friends and of course the Braydans said yes and to drive safely. You could hear the girl's shrieks echo down the church hallway as they ran off with excitement.

With hand outstretched toward Betty, Dr. Braydan said, "Well honey, are you ready to go to lunch?"

"I sure am sweetie, let's go. I'm so glad the girls are able to join us today. The prayer over them was so perfect and I believe God is going to bless them all and give them their hearts' desire. The three of them wanting to do their schooling together and planning their future careers together is just so wonderful. We were only blessed with one child and I always wanted Faith to have siblings and God is being faithful by giving her sisters in Christ. We are all so blessed!"

"I agree!" said Dr. Braydan.

They held hands as they walked out of the sanctuary and headed to their car. The weather was starting to clear up a bit; the rain had ceased, and the sun was partially peeking through the clouds. As they approached the car Dr. Braydan reached for the door handle so he could let Betty get in.

"Thank you honey," said Betty, as she got in the car.

"You're very welcome," he replied.

As they drove off, the two of them discussed how much they enjoyed the service. They also talked about how they couldn't wait for news from the college applications.

"It sure looks busy here today," said Dr. Braydan, as they parked the car in the Outback parking lot.

"It sure does," Betty replied," I wonder if the girls got a table."

Right then Dr. Braydan's phone buzzed. As he looked at it the message read, *We got a table, come toward the right side when you walk in, love you.* "They got a table," he told Betty, "how's that for service?" he said with a smile on his face.

"Perfect, I'm hungry!" she answered. "Mmm do you smell that? It smells so good! I'm definitely ordering steak."

"Me too," replied Dr. Braydan.

As they approached the table, they noticed that the girls had their coffee and water ordered and waiting for them.

"Thank you for ordering our drinks Faith," said Dad.

"Oh, you're welcome, Dad."

The waitress soon approached, and they were able to place their orders. As they sat waiting for their food to arrive, they got to talk with the girls about graduation plans. They spoke about acceptance letters and how they should be arriving soon and also about the graduation ceremony, parties, etc. The girls were very jovial as they discussed their plans. Not much time passed, and the food arrived. About halfway through the meal Dr. Braydan's phone buzzed again. It was the hospital and one of his patients had taken a turn for the worse.

Looking at Betty he says, "It's the hospital, I have to go."

"I'll go with you," she replies, as she stands up.

"Ok honey sounds good. Faith I'm sorry we have to leave, here's the money for lunch," he says, as he hands it to Faith.

Faith expressed that it was okay, and they understood duty calls. Denise and Marcie thanked the Braydans for lunch. The Braydans left and the girls continued eating. The girls were having a great time when all of a sudden they hear, "Hey Faith, how are you?" When they looked up, they saw it was Danny, Brandon, and Nicole from the hospital.

"Hi you guys, I'm good. Would you like to join us?"

"Sure, thanks," they answer, as they sit down. "How are you two?" they ask, as they look at Denise and Marcie.

"Doing good thanks," they reply.

"Are you sure we're not intruding?" asked Danny.

"No, not at all," replied Faith. "Dad got called into the hospital and Mom decided to go with him so we definitely have room for you guys."

"Ok, perfect," said Nicole, as the three of them sat down.

The waitress noticed them joining Faith and her friends, so she came over and asked if they wanted to order anything.

"We sure do," Brandon answered.

They quickly picked out what they wanted from the menu and in a few minutes the waitress went to put in their order. The six of them talked about working at the hospital and how much fun they'll all have in the years to come. Danny, Brandon, and Nicole are only about four to five years older than Faith and her friends, so they know this provides them with an opportunity to work together for many years. Having friends at work really helps to make for an enjoyable working environment and they're all looking forward to that.

Danny brought up the topic of college acceptance letters and asked if they would be coming soon. The girls excitedly answered and said they hoped so. Denise blurted out that they better get accepted. The group of friends reassured the girls that they would and when they do get accepted they should all come out and celebrate. "Yes!" was heard around the table. Plans were set; now they just had to wait for the letters to arrive.

As they continued enjoying their food and fellowship, they all made sure to update their phone contacts so that none of them would miss out on the celebration. A text message would be sent out confirming the details of the dinner, such as date, time, and place.

"This is going to be so much fun," said Faith. "Thank you guys so much for encouraging us and for helping us at the hospital. Hands-on experiences really help us to understand just how the different fields of medicine work together so perfectly."

"You're very welcome," they said." We're glad to help out."

"It wasn't long ago we were in your shoes," said Danny, "so we really do understand what you'll be going through."

"That's true, if you ever feel overwhelmed, make sure you talk to us and we'll help in any way we can," said Nicole.

"We really appreciate that," replied Marcie, as the girls nodded their head in agreement.

"Glad to be of assistance," Danny said, as he chuckled a bit.

"Alright what's so funny Danny?" asked Brandon.

"Well, I was just picturing Marcie in prison orange. We can all help out when it comes to anatomical or medical care questions, but seriously Marcie for your own sake please don't ask any of us about any law-related questions because we have no idea about that!" he laughed.

"True, if you don't want to get into trouble leave those questions to someone else!" said Brandon.

"We can, however, introduce you to our good friend Paula who does know about that stuff and I'm sure she would help you in that area," said Danny.

"Thanks for the warning, no asking you all for legal advice," Marcie laughed, "but I may take you up on introducing me to Paula, that would be great!"

"This was really fun," said Faith. "I'm so glad you guys walked in today and could join us for lunch."

They all agreed it was a very nice, impromptu, visit and it worked out perfectly. They talked about what everyone had planned for the rest of the day and it consisted of household chores, errands, and then the three girls looked at each other and laughed as they said in harmony, "homework!" They all shared a good laugh as they got up and walked out of the restaurant. When they reached the parking lot, they expressed their good-byes and left.

Chapter 5

The school year is going by pretty fast and the girls are expecting the results of their college applications to come in the mail today. They can hardly concentrate on what the teacher is discussing in class because their minds are so preoccupied with the results of the Mass State letters. The anticipation is growing by the second as they watch the clock tick in what seems to be slow motion. It feels as though time is standing still while they wait for school to be dismissed. As the bell rings, the girls grab their things, and they are off to see if their letters have indeed arrived. You can hear the girls yelling to each other as they run down the hall, "Call as soon as you know." "Ok," they answer back to one another.

Faith gets to her house first since she lives the closest to the school; almost afraid to look inside she cracks open the mailbox just a bit and peeks in. With her heart feeling as if it's going to jump right out of her chest she takes a breath, reaches in, and pulls out the mail. She can see the corner of an envelope sticking out from the middle of the pile; it has a large MS custom stamp on it. With a lump in her throat, she swallows hard. As her hands are shaking with excitement she pulls that envelope to the top of the pile and just stares at it, knowing that she holds a piece of paper that will affect her future. She stands still and ponders the thought of opening the envelope, when all of a sudden her phone rings; it's Denise and Marcie doing a three-way call with her.

"Hello," says Faith.

"Did you get it?" Faith hears Denise and Marcie screaming into the phone.

"Yea I did," Faith replies, "I'm standing here shaking, afraid to open it."

"Oh my goodness, us too!" they exclaim.

"Ok wait," Denise said." Don't open it. We'll be right over, and we'll open them together."

"Sounds great, I can't do this without you two," she replies.

On our way, see you in a few, is all Faith heard before the line went silent. The girls were on their way to Faith's house. It was finally here, the moment they've been waiting for and it is only fitting that they find out together. Faith went into the house, placed the envelope on the sofa table, and went to the kitchen to get the girls a soda out of the fridge. She paced back and forth from the kitchen to the front door waiting for the girls to get there. As she passed by the sofa table in the living room she couldn't help but look at the envelope, wondering what news it contained. Once again it felt as if time was standing still. The answer to her life goal was laying there just a few feet away. Boom, boom, boom, she heard, as the girls had arrived, and they were pounding on the front door.

"Come on in," Faith yelled, as she headed toward the door.

"Can you believe they're finally here?" Denise and Marcie screamed, as they ran in and hugged Faith.

"Not really," said Faith, as they walked into the living room. Faith picked up her envelope off the sofa table and said, "It almost feels like a dream. So how should we do this? Should we all open at the same time or each individually?"

"At the same time," said Denise, "but we need to open someone else's not our own, so pass your envelope to the left and we will all break the seal simultaneously. When we're ready we'll pull out the letter, take a breath, and start reading it out loud."

"Perfect," said Faith and Marcie.

"Ok, here we go," they said in harmony.

It was as if the opening of the envelopes were being amplified by a microphone. The sound of the paper separating from itself and then the letter being pulled out from its neatly packed pouch echoed in the quiet of the house. Their hearts were beating so hard in their chests it was as if you could hear them too. They were all set, ready to read the results. They all looked at each other, took a breath and started reading aloud.

"Dear…We are happy to inform you that you have been accepted. We got in they all started screaming!" With tears falling down their cheeks they hugged and danced and celebrated with shouts of joy. "Thank you Jesus!" they shouted. "We did it!" they exclaimed. Falling into the couch with genuine relief they couldn't stop smiling and screaming.

"I can't wait to tell my parents," said Faith.

"I know me either," said Denise, "all of our parents are going to be so happy."

"That's for sure," said Marcie, "woo hoo we got some celebrating to do!"

"Yes we do," said Faith and Denise.

"Ok, well there's no way I can wait for my parents to get off of work to tell them and I don't really want to just call or text them, so what should we do?" Faith asked.

"Road trip," yelled Denise, "let's go to each set of parents and tell them together."

"Sounds like fun!" said Faith and Marcie. "Let's do it!"

The girls gathered their things, letters in tow, and headed off to tell the parents. First stop was at Denise's house. The girls got out of the car, ran up to the house, and as soon as they got through the front door Denise started hollering for her mom and dad.

"Mom, Dad, you home?"

"In the kitchen sweetie," they yell back.

The three girls ran to the kitchen bursting with excitement.

"Hello girls," said Denise's parents.

"Hello Mr. and Mrs. Ruken," said Faith and Marcie.

"What's going on with you three today?" asked the Rukens.

"Oh, just a little news," said Denise, as she held up her acceptance letter.

"Is that what we think it is?" her parents asked. By this time Denise's parents are standing by the girls and reaching for the letter.

Denise playfully holds the letter away from them while saying, "Oh is this something you want to see?" she giggles.

"Yes please," says her mom, as she grabs for the letter while her dad stands by and laughs at their playfulness.

As her parents read the letter, they can't help but get emotional, "congratulations sweetie," they say as they embraced Denise. "We are so proud of you honey."

"Thanks you guys. We all got in and we want to tell it together, so is it ok if I go with Faith and Marcie, to tell their parents?" asked Denise.

"Congratulations girls," they said, as they turned to hug Faith and Marcie." Of course it's ok for you to go with them; you girls have fun."

"Thanks," the girls replied, and in a moment the three of them were off to tell Marcie's parents.

As they drive towards Marcie's house they talk about how much fun they're having. As soon as they pull up the driveway they see Marcie's parents outside working on the landscape; they park the car, get out, and run towards them.

"Mom, Dad!" shouts Marcie.

"Hey honey, what are you guys up to?" they ask.

"Well, I have something to tell you, do you have a minute?"

"Of course honey, is everything ok?" they ask, as they wipe off their hands on a cloth.

"Umm yea I would say so," said Marcie, as she hands them the letter.

"What's this?" they ask, as they unfold the letter and in about a second, they both start screaming. "Congratulations honey, we're so proud of you!"

"Thanks guys, I'm a little excited too! We all are because we all got in!"

"Oh that's great news, congratulations girls," said the Lindens.

"Thanks Mr. and Mrs. Linden," the girls respond.

"Have you told your parents yet?"

"One more set to go," said Faith. "My parents are still at work and I can't wait for them to get home, so I want to go tell them now."

"That's understandable," said Marcie's mom, "it's very exciting news."

"Mom, we really want to do this together, so is it ok if I go with them?" asked Marcie.

"Yes, of course!"

"Thanks Mom," said Marcie.

"Once again the girls found themselves riding in the car on a mission to share their news.

"This is so much fun," said Faith. "I'm so glad we did this together, it really has made it so much more special. You two are the sisters I never had but always wanted. I thank God for you both."

"We feel the same way," said Denise and Marcie.

As the girls arrived at the hospital parking lot they started to scream, parked the car and jumped out. The three of them ran toward the door as fast as they could. Faith grabbed the handle on the door, swung it open, and the girls hurried through the halls looking for Faith's parents. When they arrived on the 4th floor they spotted the Braydans walking down the hallway. Faith yelled out to her parents. When the Braydans turned around they saw the three girls rushing toward them.

"Hello girls, what are you three up to?" they ask.

Faith reaching the letter towards them says, "Well this came today."

Dr. and Mrs. Braydan both reach toward the letter to grab it, but Faith playfully pulls it away from them.

"Is it" was all they got out of their mouths before all three of the girls yelled, "Yes it is!" The Braydans again started to say, "well what's the" when again the girls interrupted with shouts of, "We got in. All of us!"

"Oh honey, we are so happy for you and so very proud of you," the Braydans told Faith, as they hugged her. Then turning to the other girls, they also expressed their proud feelings and congratulations to them.

"This calls for a celebration!" exclaimed Dr. Braydan.

"I couldn't agree more," said Nurse Betty.

"Sounds great, what do you have in mind?" asked Faith.

"Dinner for sure tonight, let's meet 6 o'clock at Outback," said Dad. "Did you girls tell your parents yet?"

"Yes we did," the girls answered. "We went by our houses before we came here with Faith to tell you and Mrs. Braydan."

"Perfect, that means your parents are home. Girls I want you to call your parents and invite them to join us; it's only right that we all celebrate together," said Dr. Braydan. "Oh, and it's our treat! I'll call and make a reservation for all of us. In fact, didn't Brandon, Nicole, and Danny want to celebrate when you got your acceptance letters?" he asked, as he turned toward Faith.

"Yes they did," answered Faith.

"Ok, then you better text them and have them meet us there also. Oh, and don't forget Grandma Martha," said Dad.

"Ok Dad, I'm on it. This is going to be so much fun! Thanks Dad," said Faith.

"Yes, thank you so much Dr. Braydan!" said the girls. "We'll get ahold of our parents right away."

"It's our pleasure girls," said the Braydans. "We'll see you all at Outback."

The Braydans hugged the girls, said good-bye and went on to finish their work for the day. The girls took off with their phones in hand making calls and sending texts.

Six o'clock arrived fast and they all made their way to the restaurant. The Braydans arrived first and had the table all set up with balloons and other decorations to make it very festive. As the guests approached the table the excitement became palpable. Hugs and congratulations were being exchanged amongst the group. The girls were all smiles as they visited with everyone. Talks of their future plans filled the air when all of a sudden, a tinkling sound of a glass being tapped with silverware was heard by all.

Dr. Braydan standing with a glass in hand and raised in the air started to say, "I'd like to thank everyone for coming out tonight to celebrate this very special occasion with us. We are so proud of the girls getting into Mass State and we look forward to celebrating many of their accomplishments together with all of you. So, cheers to the girls and their futures. We pray that God Blesses them by leading them in every step they take, and may they be a blessing to all of those that He puts in their path, congratulations again girls!"

"To the girls," the rest join in saying, as they raise their glasses and smile in agreement to the blessing.

With that being said the girls stood up.

Faith raised her glass and said, "On behalf of the girls and me we'd like to thank you all so much. Dad, Mom, thank you for pulling this all together it really does mean a lot to us. We couldn't imagine life without you all in it. This day has worked out perfectly. Everyone that was invited was able to attend and we don't take that for granted. We're able to feel the love and support from every one of you. This is a monumental moment in our lives, and we realize just how blessed we are to have family and friends to share this moment with us. So, thanks again."

"Here, here" was being shouted out, as glasses were being clinked together and the celebration continued on.

Faith's Locket

Karen Young

Chapter 6

A couple months have passed by and graduation day is quickly approaching. The girls' plans and dreams are on course and they couldn't be more elated. Parties are in the planning process and the excitement at school is palpable. The tight knit community of Bayside seems to be bursting forth with a spirit of celebration. While the graduating class feels some sense of sadness with the closing of this chapter in their lives, they can't deny the enthusiasm they feel as they are ready to birth a new chapter. It has been announced that Faith is the Valedictorian of her graduating class. This honor is awarded to the student with the highest academic achievements and the Braydans couldn't be prouder that Faith has obtained this honor. Denise and Marcie are so happy for Faith, but they are not surprised that this honor is bestowed upon their dear friend. They couldn't imagine anyone else holding that position. Of course, with news of this special recognition, a graduation outfit shopping excursion has been put into motion.

Within seconds after the chiming of the school dismissal bell, you can hear the buzzing of the cell phone text messaging alerts going off on the girl's phones.

Ok girls are we ready to shop? wrote Faith.

Absolutely! replied Denise.

Yes! Marcie responded.

Ok meet me in the parking lot and we'll all ride together, wrote Faith.

Perfect! Denise signed off with a happy face.

See you there! Marcie responded with an emoji of a girl running.

As the girls were approaching Faith's car, you could hear the exuberance in their voices as they shouted out to one another.

"Can you believe we graduate in two weeks?" said Faith.

"Not really, it felt like this day was so far away and now it's nearly here," replied Denise, "it's kind of unbelievable."

"Right," Marcie chimed in, "it's incredible."

"Ok well, another unbelievable thing is we have to find outfits for graduation day and outfits for our graduation parties, so girls get your game face on and let's do this. Are you with me?" jokes Faith.

Denise and Marcie start laughing as they respond, "Oh yea! We're with you! Look out stores…here we come!"

The girls hopped into Faith's car and off they went. The day was warm and beautiful, a perfect day to make memories with special friends. As they drove through the town, they couldn't help but notice how the local stores had put up decorations for the graduating class. Signs were on the store front windows wishing the graduating class great success. Some were simple signs with basic congratulations, while others consisted of deeper messages like prayers. What a blessing to grow up in a community that is not ashamed to show love and support to the youth of their town. The girls felt a sense of gratitude as they noticed the kindnesses expressed by the people in their community. They didn't take this kindness for granted. They made a special effort to express their thanks to the many stores that were so gracious to take the time out to put up these special messages. The girls purposely stopped at each location to say "Thank You" to the store owners. The day turned out to be very successful; within four hours each girl found and purchased the perfect outfit for each occasion. Tired and hungry, the girls decided to grab a quick bite to eat. When they had finished eating, they headed back to the school so Denise and Marcie could get their cars. As they approached the school parking lot, they discussed how happy they were that they all found their outfits and also how excited they are to show them to their moms.

"Well, here we are girls, it was so fun," said Faith, as she parked next to Denise and Marcie's cars.

"It really was," they replied, as they got out and started to transfer their shopping bags into their own cars.

The girls exchanged their good-byes and headed to their respective homes.

The sun was starting to set by this time and the sky was illuminated with the most beautiful colors. The smells of spring filled the evening air making it a perfect ending to a most enjoyable day. Faith knew that this was a day she would never forget. Her mind wandered as she drove home. She could hardly wait to arrive because she was so excited to show her outfits to her mom. As she approached her house her cell phone buzzed. She pulled up the driveway, proceeded to park her car, looked at her phone, and chuckled as she read, *When you coming home?* It was a text from her mom. *Just pulled in the driveway,* Faith responded. *Open the door please. It was a very successful shopping excursion.*

Oh no, Mom responded with an emoji to match, then another of, *just kidding* and a smiling/crying emoji.

Faith laughed as she looked at the messages. Walking toward the front door she sees her mom standing there with the door open, waiting for her to come in.

Mom hollers, "Do you need help carrying the bags in?"

"I got them," Faith yells back. "Thanks for opening the door," she said, as she got closer.

"You're welcome baby. I can't wait to see what you bought!"

"Where's Dad?" asked Faith.

"He's in his study. Let's go to your room so you can show me your outfits. We'll let Dad see them in a bit."

"Ok. I'm really excited to show them to you!"

Faith and her mom went to Faith's room, bags in tow giggling with excitement. The joy they were feeling was undeniable. Mother and daughter were making memories and enjoying every moment. Ooh's and aah's were being expressed as each outfit was shown, one just as beautiful as the one before it.

"You made some stunning choices," said Mom.

"Thanks, I'm so glad you like them. I still have to pick out accessories though. Do you think you can help me do that?"

"Absolutely baby, I would be honored. Now that they're all displayed on the bed let's have your dad come see them."

"Sounds great," Faith said, as she sprinted out the bedroom and hollered for her dad.

"Dad...can you come up here for a moment?"

"Sure honey, be right up," he yells back.

When Dr. Braydan entered the room he looked at Faith, he chuckled and asked, "Does the store have anything left?"

"Ha ha very funny Dad," Faith smiled.

"Well, I can see you made some beautiful choices and I'm sure you're going to be the loveliest girl at graduation."

"Awe, thanks Dad, that's very sweet of you to say."

"Just truth sweetheart, stating facts is all," he looks at her with adoration.

"James, Faith asked me to help her pick out accessories to go with the outfits," says Mom, as she winks.

"Oh did she?" he responds with a smirk on his face.

"Hey, wait a minute what's that winking about and that smirk?" asks Faith.

"Excuse me one minute," says Dad, as he leaves the room and goes into his bedroom.

"What is it?" Faith asks, as she looks at her mom.

"You'll see," she responds.

"Sweetheart," Dad says, as he reenters Faith's room," Mom and I got this for you, and we hope that you like it. We figured you could wear it with your outfits."

Faith could feel a lump developing in her throat and tears welling up in her eyes as she reaches to receive the box that her Dad is presenting to her. She opens it up and gasps.

"This is perfect! It's so beautiful! Thank you both so much!" she exclaims, as she leans in to hug them.

"You're welcome, we love you very much sweetheart," they reply, as they embrace her.

Faith looks at the necklace closer and discovers that it's a locket. As she opens it up to look inside, she has a confused look on her face. The locket is empty. Looking toward her parents she asks, "Why is it empty?"

"It's your locket baby to fill with what you choose," Mom replies.

"Mom and I discussed it many times whether we should be the ones to pick out what to put inside it but it's not ours to fill sweetheart so we're leaving it up to you. Every heart holds deep secrets, private desires, love, hopes, and beliefs. What one puts in their own locket is very personal. It should only be chosen by the one who wears it."

"Don't feel pressured to fill it right away. There is no right or wrong thing to put in it. When the time is right you will know without a shadow of a doubt exactly what should go inside," said Mom.

"Thanks again you guys, I love it! I will be patient and wait for the right and perfect thing to put inside it, I promise."

"We're so glad you like it sweetheart," they said, as they hug her again.

"We better let you work on getting these clothes hung up and put away, so we'll say good night," said Mom.

"Ok guys, sleep good," Faith says, as she embraces them one more time.

Faith started picking up her clothes and hanging them up as her parents headed toward their bedroom. Thoughts of her beautiful locket and the possible contents flowed through her mind. What will fill her locket she wonders? Should she put a picture of her parents in it? Will it hold a picture of a great love? Faith finished putting her things away; then as she lied down on her bed she drifted off to sleep, dreaming of what might possibly fill her locket.

Faith's Locket

Chapter 7

It's almost here! The graduating class is counting down the last few days of their high school experience. The halls of the school are filled with conversations of party plans and college commitments. The girls have all their plans set and everything is moving at what feels like warp speed. It seems like yesterday that the girls had just started high school and now they are about to complete it and move on to college. What once was just a thought, a mere goal, is now full-blown reality.

All of a sudden, a school wide announcement is broadcast. "Attention Seniors, this is your principal speaking, I'd like to first congratulate you on your upcoming graduation, but I also want to inform you that your caps and gowns have arrived and are now ready to be picked up. Teachers, please dismiss your seniors from class so they can come to the auditorium and pick up their garments. Thank you." Within moments you could hear books slamming shut, doors closing, feet running down the halls, and shouts of joy echoing off the walls.

The line of students in the auditorium assembled quickly. Denise arrived first and got in line; she was anxiously looking around as she waited for Marcie and Faith to get there. When she saw them enter the auditorium, she shouted out to them and waved her hands up in the air to get them to come join her in line; they quickly rushed to her side. As they stood there waiting for the line to advance, they talked about how thrilled they were that the caps and gowns had arrived that day. The girls were to wear white and the boys were wearing red. They discussed how nice the silver and gold honor cords would look with both colors of gowns.

Eventually talks shifted to what they had to do that afternoon. Denise was going shopping for decorations with her mom, Marcie was going to be helping her mom prep things around the house for her party, and Faith was scheduled to volunteer at the hospital.

As the girls approached the table where they were handing out the caps and gowns, the ladies there, asked for their names. The girls proudly stated, "Faith Braydan, Denise Ruken, and Marcie Linden."

Ok here you go girls," the ladies said, as they handed them their packages.

The girls gladly received their items as they proudly started walking away with their caps and gowns in tow. There was an undeniable feeling of closure and adventure all at the same time. One season of life was about to end, but another was about to begin.

"Well, this is it girls," said Faith, "Saturday will be here before you know it and we'll be graduating."

"I can't wait," said Denise. "It's been a long time coming."

"Yea, but now looking back on it, it went fast," said Marcie.

"It's been quite a journey so far, but on the other hand our journey's only beginning," replied Faith.

"Is that part of your Valedictorian speech Faith?" Denise jokes.

"Ha ha funny, but hey it is pretty good, I might have to use it," Faith laughs.

Before they knew it, they had arrived at their cars in the school parking lot. The girls hugged each other, said their good-byes, and then they scattered, heading in different directions to attend to the tasks they had to complete that day.

Faith headed to the hospital. As she drove many thoughts were whirling in her mind; thoughts of the past school years, thoughts of all the upcoming events, and thoughts of what she might actually say in her speech. It wasn't long at all and Faith found herself pulling into the hospital parking lot. When she looked at the hospital, she couldn't help but feel a sense of gratitude that her life was turning out so well. She sat there for a moment as her heart went out to the people that were in there, suffering with illness or injury and she felt blessed that she was going to help them. Faith didn't want to take life for granted and she wanted to always put God first and give him honor for all He has done. As she sat in her car she bowed her head and said, "Lord, I thank you for your faithfulness. Use me Lord to help those in need, give me words that I may speak to the hurting and grant healing to those that need it. In Jesus' name I pray. Amen." With her heart full of compassion, she got out of her car and walked to the entrance of the hospital. When she was approaching the door Clem and Phillip noticed her coming; they quickly pushed open the doors and let her walk in.

"Hello Faith," they said. "Good to see you."

"Hi Clem, Hi Phillip," she responded. "Good to see you as well and thanks for opening the door for me."

"It's our pleasure Faith."

Hilda and Florence were also there and greeted Faith as she walked in. Faith politely said hello but she was running a bit behind so she couldn't take the time to talk. She quickly headed toward the elevator; the door promptly opened and she was able to step right in. Once inside she pressed button 2 and was on her way up to the second floor. As the doors opened she stepped out and walked toward the nurses' desk. Upon arrival she grabbed the clipboard as usual and checked to see what her schedule entailed for the day. As she scanned through the document she noticed a repeat patient. She quickly went to her locker to drop off her personal belongings and then she was off to start her shift.

Knock, knock she said, as she entered Room 221. Pulling back the curtain she playfully peeked in at Jettie and his wife Lillie.

"Hello you two," she said, as she walked to the bedside.

"How are you doing Jettie?" she asked.

"Oh Faith, it's so good to see you. I'm doing well, or I should say as well as can be expected."

"Well that's good to hear," she replied. "I see they did another surgery on your knee."

"Yea, when you get old like me things start to fall apart," he replied.

"Oh nonsense. You're not old; you're mature," she says with a grin.

"Ha ha, is that what you kids are calling it these days? Hey, I hear you're going into Mass State's physical therapy program."

"Yes, that's correct. I'll be able to help you a lot more in the future once I'm trained in that specialty."

"Good to know," said Jettie.

"Yes, we will be requesting you as our therapist for every procedure we have after you get certified," said Lillie.

"Awe, that's so sweet. It will be my honor to take care of you both anytime," she said, as she adjusted Jettie's pillow and blanket. "Can I get either of you anything? Would you like a drink, something to eat, or maybe something to read?"

"No, we're fine, but thank you," Jettie replied. "I could use some prayers though."

"I'm on it as usual. You know me Jettie, I love to pray for my patients and even more so when I know the patients want me to. God is so faithful to us and I know that He will help your healing process be quick and you'll be up and about soon. He does not leave us nor forsake us. He loves us so very much. We must believe in Him."

"Amen," replied Jettie and Lillie.

"Ok, well it was great to see you two. Just press the call button if you need anything," said Faith, as she walked out of the room to go check on the next patient.

Faith's day seemed to be going by very fast. When she looked at her watch she could hardly believe that three hours had already passed. Her shift was just about over but she had one more patient to check in on, Room 423. When she arrived at the entrance of the room she paused and lightly knocked on the door before going in.

"Hello," said Faith, as she approached the bedside.

"Yea, what do you want?" asked the man lying in the bed.

"I just wanted to ask if there was anything I could do for you."

With a snarling look the man said, "Can you get me out of here?"

"Well, that depends on what you mean by get you out of here," she replied with a smile on her face. "If you're asking if I can discharge you the answer would be I'm sorry, but I cannot do that. If you're asking me to take you out of your room for a walk or a stroll in a wheelchair, I can ask your nurse and see what she says."

"You would do that for me?"

"Of course I would," Faith replied.

"I would like very much to get out of this room by any means possible."

"Ok then, I'll be back in a moment; I'll go ask your nurse what's allowed."

In a flash Faith left Room 423 and headed to the nurses' station. While she was there the nurse did give her permission to take the man for a walk, but he had to be in a wheelchair. With an extra pep in her step Faith went and got a wheelchair from the storage closet and quickly went back to share the good news. She was so happy that the nurse gave her permission to fulfill the man's simple request that she found herself humming as she walked. Sometimes it's the little things that make the biggest impact.

Arriving back at the room with wheelchair in tow, Faith pulled back the curtain with a smile on her face and said, "You ready to go for a ride?"

The man's face lit up like it was Christmas. "Really?" he said, with such enthusiasm.

"Yes," Faith replied. "We have a green light from your nurse, so let's get going. Oh, and by the way, my name is Faith."

"It's nice to meet you Faith; my name is Henry. Thank you so much for doing this for me. I know that I didn't speak to you in the best tone when you first entered my room and I'm sorry for that."

"It's okay Henry and I must say it's very nice to meet you as well. Now let's get you in this chair and we'll get started on our adventure."

"Sounds great," said Henry.

In a few moments Faith had Henry securely placed in the wheelchair and they were on their way. Henry was not allowed to go outside of the hospital, but other than that the nurse didn't give any other restrictions, so Faith was able to take him on a long journey. They went to many different floors of the hospital. She took Henry to an area that provided a beautiful view of the Bay; they sat there for quite a while and enjoyed the view of the sun glistening on the water as the boats sailed around. Henry shared stories with Faith about his life and things that he has gone through. She sat patiently and listened to every word. Henry may have seemed angry and bitter when Faith first entered his room but really Henry was just lonely. Faith's kindness was really the medicine he needed. After they were finished with their excursion, Faith took Henry back to his room and got him safely back into his bed.

"Well Henry, I really enjoyed spending time with you, but my shift is over. I have to get home, complete my homework and go to school in the morning, so I must say good-bye for now."

"Thank you so much Faith for showing such kindness to an old geezer like me."

"It was my pleasure Henry," Faith laughed "and you're not an old geezer. You're a very nice older gentleman whom I'm glad to have had the opportunity to meet and spend some time with. Hopefully I will see you again."

"I would like that very much," he replied. "Have a great evening."

"Thank you, you as well," said Faith, as she walked out of his room.

Chapter 8

Graduation Day has finally arrived. The clear blue sky with the sun shining beautifully today is making it a perfect day to have an outside graduation ceremony. The stage is set and the chairs have been placed on the school lawn where the ceremony is scheduled to take place. The trees and flowers in full bloom are painting the landscape in a breathtaking spectrum of colors. The aroma from the flowers is only adding to the ambiance making the surroundings absolutely elegant. The Braydans like all the other families that have a graduate in their household are busy getting ready for this highly anticipated and most exciting day.

"Faith," her mother yells up the stairs, "are you going to eat anything this morning?"

"I'm not sure Mom," she answers, "I'm so nervous about the speech I don't know if I can."

"You'll do great baby and I really think you need to eat a little something. I'll bring you up some juice, some fruit, and a bagel."

"Ok Mom," Faith replied.

Faith continued to get things organized for the day as her mom prepared her food. After it was ready her mom brought the food upstairs to Faith as she said she would. While walking up the stairs and then down the hallway toward Faiths room her mom could hear Faith practicing her speech.

"Sounds great honey, you're going to do an amazing job," said Mom, as she entered Faith's room and placed the plate of food on the dresser.

"Thanks Mom, for the food and for the support. You and Dad have always been here for me, believing in me, I just don't know what I'd do without you."

"You're welcome honey, we don't plan on going anywhere; we'll always be here for you if we can help it. Now take a minute and eat a bit. I'm going to go back downstairs and clean up the kitchen before I start getting ready for the ceremony." Pausing at the doorway Mom looked back at Faith and said, "I love you very much Faith and I'm just so proud of you."

"I love you too Mom and thanks for everything."

Faith picked up the plate of food and started eating as her mom walked out of the room. Within seconds after Betty exited Faith's room, tears started to roll down her face as she envisioned her little girl all grown up and preparing to not only graduate from high school, but to have the honor of being Valedictorian. It was almost too good to be true.

As Betty reached the bottom of the staircase James met her there. Smiling at her he gently reached his hand to her face and wiped away her tears.

"I love you Betty," he said. "It's going to be a great day. We have so much to be thankful for."

"I love you too," she replied. "And yes we sure do."

The two of them went to the kitchen and finished cleaning it up. Quickly after that they were in their room getting ready for the festivities. They could hear Faith rushing around in her room getting ready as well. They could also hear jovial screams every now and again as Faith was on a three-way call with Denise and Marcie. These girls always find a way to be together, if not in person then by phone or computer. After a while, Faith and the girls ended their call so they could all finish getting ready.

"Faith," Dad yelled, "are you almost ready honey? We don't want to be late."

"Absolutely Dad, I'll be right there."

Faith quickly finished getting ready by putting on the lovely locket that her parents had bought her. She paused, looked around her room, grabbed her speech, and sighed. She couldn't help but think when she returned from the ceremony that things would feel different. Somehow in a matter of hours she would feel older. She grasped her locket as it hung around her neck and she rubbed it gently between her fingers. Her youthful life was being left behind and her path to adulthood was in front of her. As she stepped out of her room she adjusted her cap and gown and started to go down the stairs. Her parents were standing at the bottom of the staircase looking up at their precious daughter. Their faces were glowing as they gazed upon their child.

"Oh honey, you look so beautiful," they said.

"Thanks guys."

"So, are you ready to do this?" Dad asked.

"Definitely," Faith replied.

"Ok then ladies, let's go!"

Dr. Braydan held the door open as the loves of his life headed toward the car. He couldn't help but smile at them, his heart full of love and respect.

"Hold on one moment," he said to them, "let me get the car doors for you two."

Mrs. Braydan and Faith paused and allowed him to be the gentleman that he was as they let him open the car doors. After they were both seated, Dr. Braydan closed their doors and quickly made his way around the car and sat in the driver's seat.

"Buckle up," he said, as he glanced at both of them," you know my precious cargo is in this car. I love you both so very much."

"We love you too," they replied.

The drive to the school was extremely pleasant. The town never looked lovelier. Every color of the rainbow seemed to be bursting forth on this most glorious day. "Congratulations Graduate" signs were displayed everywhere. Cars were coming from every direction trying to make their way to the school. When they arrived, the parking lot was almost full.

"Wow look at this turn out," Mom said.

"With weather like this I think everyone is attending," said Dad.

"Oh no," said Faith, "I'm getting nervous. I hope I don't mess up my speech."

"You're going to do fine sweetheart, whatever you say will be perfect."

"Thanks Dad, that means a lot."

As Dr. Braydan was parking the car, Faith spotted Denise and Marcie just a few spaces down. Her heart started to pound even faster than before. The excitement was building. Denise and Marcie noticed the Braydan's car, so they started to run toward it. Faith could hardly wait for her dad to put the car in park. She flung the door open, jumped out of the car, and the girlish screams filled the air. The parents gathered around and just smiled. In moments they all started walking toward the ceremony location. The girls paused, hugged their parents, and then they proceeded to check in so they could get lined up for the processional. The parents had to quickly choose their seats and then anxiously wait for the ceremony to start. The crowd that gathered was one of largest the school has ever had. Grandma Martha, many friends from the church, and friends from the hospital started to fill up the rows of seats surrounding the Braydans.

"Thank you all for coming," the Braydans said. "It really is so nice of you. Faith is going to be so surprised."

"We wouldn't miss it," they replied.

All of a sudden the music started to play. The crowd turned around and looked toward the back. The students were all lined up and ready for the processional to start. Tears began to well up in the eyes of many as they gazed upon the graduates. This moment is a time that will forever be in the hearts of the graduates and their loved ones. They looked absolutely regal in their caps and gowns as they walked gracefully down the aisles. Pictures were being taken from every direction, people trying to freeze in time this most precious of moments. The graduates arrived at their seats and the ceremony began. The Master of Ceremonies walked to the podium, turned on the microphone, and addressed all that had gathered there. After a few special speakers had completed their part in the ceremony, it was time for Faith to give her speech. The Master of Ceremonies once again approached the podium; with a smile on his face, he proceeded to introduce Faith.

"It is with great honor that I get to introduce to you a very special young lady that has lived her whole life here in Bayside. She and her family are a vital part of our community. She has always been an exceptional student and an asset to our school. She has also always been very active in many of our school clubs and volunteered for numerous school events. It is no surprise that she has achieved the highest academic GPA in this class. I am so proud to present to you, your Valedictorian, Faith Braydan."

The crowd erupted with clapping, whistling, and shouting. The support she received was overwhelming. Faith smiled, stood up, and proceeded to the stage. When she made it to the podium she shook the hand of the MC, thanked him, and then adjusted the mic.

"First of all, I'd like to thank God for this beautiful day. I'd also like to thank you all for that warm welcome and for taking time out of your day to celebrate with all of us graduates. It is with a humble heart that I receive this honor that is bestowed upon me today. We have all worked so very hard to accomplish our goals. We don't take for granted the many blessings we have here in this great country and mostly here in this amazing community. We couldn't have accomplished our goals without the support of our many family members and friends and we want you to know how important you all are to us. From all the graduates to all of you, we love you!"

"To my fellow graduates, I am honored to be up here to represent our incredible class. We are like one big happy family living in an ideal place. The road ahead of us may take us in many different directions but the ties that bind us will remain strong and everlasting. Space may divide us in mileage but the love of one another closes that gap. Always remember the values you have grown up with here in Bayside and spread those values to your new communities in which you end up in, that way we can do our part to better this world in which we live. Be a light in the dark spaces and exude the kindness you have been taught by living here. We can make a difference in this world. I was talking to a couple friends the other day and we reflected on how we've waited for this moment for so long, but then again it has come quickly. Life has been quite a journey so far, but on the other hand our journey's only beginning. As we all move forward with more goals set before us, I know without a doubt that we can accomplish them all. I'm so very happy and blessed to have grown up with you and I look forward to continuing this journey we call life together. It is with great pleasure that I say congratulations to you all! We did it!!! Thank you and may God bless you."

    The crowd stood up and gave Faith a standing ovation. She was so relieved that the speech was over and now she could rejoin the other graduates and receive their diplomas. As she walked to her seat she could hear Denise and Marcie screaming out, we love you Faith. She smiled at them and said I love you too. Within moments the MC asked the class to stand for the receiving of diplomas. As the names were called out the graduates walked up on the stage and gladly received their diploma. Cameras were capturing the special moments and the crowd cheered loudly. At the end of the ceremony, after all the graduates had returned to their seats, the MC closed in prayer. It was a perfect ending to a wonderful ceremony.

    As the recessional song started playing, the graduates proceeded to exit. After all the graduates and faculty members had exited the ceremony area the rest of the guests were dismissed from their seats. When the Braydans reached the back of the ceremony area they immediately started to look for Faith. Faith was anxiously waiting for them. Once she saw her parents she started to run toward them. With arms wide open she grabbed and hugged them both.

"Congratulations baby," they said.

"Thanks Mom, thanks Dad," she replied.

Everyone else that came to support Faith was standing off to the side letting the Braydans have a private moment. Once that moment was done they came over to share in the celebration and give their congratulations to Faith. Hugs and laughter were being shared in abundance. Faith couldn't have been more surprised or happier at how many people turned out to support her and celebrate with her. The Braydans didn't know ahead of time how many friends were coming to the ceremony, so they didn't make any plans for a luncheon, but that wasn't going to stop Dr. Braydan from trying to pull something special together now. He counted the people, sneaked off to the side a bit, called the Olive Garden, and asked if their banquet room was available. Luckily it was, so he reserved it for 25 guests. When he rejoined the group of family and friends, he asked for everyone's attention.

"Excuse me everyone," he said, "I'd like to thank you all for coming out and supporting Faith and for celebrating with us this very special moment in her life. We are so very proud of her and well, we don't want the celebrating to end here, so we would like to invite you all to join us for lunch at the Olive Garden. I have already called and reserved the banquet room for us; it's our treat so if you would all join us we would be very pleased."

"Oh Dad, that's incredible thanks so much," said Faith, as she hugged him.

"Yes, thank you," the many friends chimed in.

"It's our pleasure," said Dr. Braydan. "We'll see you all there."

The group started to leave so they could meet up at the restaurant. The Braydans still hadn't seen Denise or Marcie and they were not going to leave without congratulating them and also inviting them to lunch. As the crowd started to disperse the Braydans spotted the Rukens and Lindens. Faith immediately ran over to where Denise and Marcie were standing with their parents; the girls immediately started to hug and scream with joy.

"Congratulations girls," the Braydans said, as they reached to hug them both.

"Thank you," they replied.

"Do you have plans for lunch?" Dr. Braydan asked the Ruken and Linden families.

"No, we didn't plan anything ahead of time," they answered.

"Perfect," said Dr. Braydan, "because I have reserved a room at the Olive Garden, and we want you all to join us there as our guests. Denise and Marcie are like sisters to Faith and it wouldn't be a complete celebration without you all there."

"That sounds great, we would love to," they replied.

"Ok well let's go, we'll see you all there," said Dr. Braydan.

Within a few moments everyone headed to their cars and they were on their way to the restaurant. When they got there and entered the banquet room the guests that had arrived before them stood up, applauded, and whistled as the graduates entered the room. A fine celebration was started, and the girls couldn't have been more appreciative or excited. It was ideal. The spontaneous gathering was just what they all needed to make the day even more special.

Chapter 9

It's hard to believe a year and a half has gone by since the girls graduated. Graduation parties are now nothing more than a treasured memory, each one as beautiful and successful as the other.

The girls are well into their programs at Mass State and they have continued with their volunteer obligations. They've learned a lot pertaining to their individual modalities and are thriving in their classes. Besides keeping up with all of their academic requirements each of the girls has gracefully accepted the opportunity to job shadow in order to be exposed to more situations that may arise in their daily duties. Kay is helping Faith, Nurse Braydan is with Denise, and Paula has been working with Marcie; the help from these women has been invaluable and the girls are grateful to have them as mentors.

Fall semester is just about over and Christmas is quickly approaching. The hustle and bustle of the holidays has everyone very busy. The community is decked out in Christmas splendor and at night the lights glisten on the snow like sparkling gems. When you walk around town you can't help but hum along to the

Christmas music that's being played over the outside speakers. All of the stores participate in decorating, so there's not a single building without lights covering it in the most beautiful display of colors. The hospital also participates in the community's tradition of decorating, and it is just glowing. Even the grounds outside are decorated so that the patients can look out their windows or go to special atrium areas and see the breathtaking beauty of the holiday season. When you enter the hospital lobby a beautifully decorated 30-foot Christmas tree is the first thing you notice. As you walk through the halls you see many poinsettias and specially decorated trees on every floor, in hopes to uplift the spirits of the patients. Of course the staff wishes that everyone would be able to spend the holidays at home, but unfortunately some patients will not get to go home during the Christmas season, so the hospital tries its best to help them enjoy the holiday with special activities and treats.

One such patient that has to be under constant care is a little girl named Hope. She has a condition that requires her to be in the hospital to receive treatments and unfortunately they won't be completed before Christmas. Faith's heart, full of compassion, has gone out to this little girl and she has become very attached to Hope. Determined to make sure that Hope has a great holiday Faith decided she's going to go in and visit with Hope even on her days off.

It was Saturday morning December 10th and Faith's phone alarm went off to the tune of "Let it Snow." Reaching over to turn it off she couldn't help but smile as she realized it was time to go visit Hope. As she got up to get ready, she could hear her parent's voices coming from downstairs. Faith quickly got dressed, grabbed a tote bag, and started gathering things. The bag got heavier and heavier as she loaded up on games and art supplies so that she and Hope would have something to do that day. In a few moments she was headed down the stairs.

"Faith breakfast is almost ready," she could hear her mom say.

"Good morning guys," Faith said, as she entered the kitchen.

"Good morning," they replied.

"What are your plans today?" Dad asked.

"I'm heading to the hospital to visit with Hope," she replied, as she grabbed a bagel and started spreading some cream cheese on it.

"Honey it's really sweet of you to spend so much time with Hope, but please be careful not to get too attached. Hope is a very sick little girl. Remember I warned you that things can happen beyond our control and well I don't want you getting hurt if something bad happens to her," said Dad.

"I know and I won't, I just feel bad that she has to be in the hospital during the holiday. She's only six years old and I just want to bring some joy into her life."

"Ok honey just guard your heart," her parents warned.

"I will," she said, as she packed up some snacks for the day and in a flash she was out the door.

As soon as Faith got in her car she put her phone on speaker and did a three-way call to Denise and Marcie. She explained to them that she was going to spend some time with Hope and asked if they would like to join her. They of course wanted to, so Faith offered to pick them up. First stop was at Denise's, then on to Marcie's. The girls were looking forward to having some down time now that the fall semester had ended and spending time together spreading cheer to Hope was just what the three of them needed. With the Christmas tunes cranking on the car radio, they headed to the hospital, singing along and laughing the whole way. Upon arriving at the hospital, they all grabbed a bag of supplies and headed in making a direct shot to Hope's room.

"Knock, knock," said Faith, as they entered.

"Hi!" said Hope, with a distinct tone of excitement in her voice.

"I brought a couple of my best friends to spend the day with us," Faith proceeded to tell Hope, as she got closer to her bedside. "Hope, this is Denise and Marcie."

Hope raised her hand and waved slightly at them.

"It's so nice to meet you Hope," they said, "and we're happy to be here."

Faith explained to Hope that she has known Denise and Marcie for most of her life. She continued talking to Hope while the girls started setting up the art supplies and games.

"So, what would you like to do today?" asked Faith. "I brought games and art supplies."

"Hmmm," said Hope, as she placed her finger up toward her face as if to be thinking hard about her answer. All of a sudden she blurted out, "let's make decorations for my room and cards for some of the patients."

"Ok, that's a great idea!"

In a matter of moments all four girls were sitting around the table making cut out snowflakes, Christmas trees, ornaments, and more. Pieces of construction paper were everywhere. They laughed and joked as they worked with glue sticks, glitter, markers, and more. What fun they were having spending quality time with this new little friend. It didn't take long before Hope's room had decorations on every wall and even on the windows. The Christmas cards were made, and it was time to deliver them. Faith got permission from the nurses to take Hope around in a wheelchair to deliver cards to the patients. "Merry Christmas" in glitter was on the front of the cards and a traced hand of Hope's was inside that showed it was indeed from a child. Hope also drew a heart on the inside of the hand and then wrote her name. In an effort to avoid germs and a desire not to bother the patients they taped the cards at the entrance of the rooms and the nurses said they would take them into the patients when they made their rounds. This was all so exciting for Hope, but it was very apparent that it was taking a toll on her energy level, so Faith, Denise, and Marcie took Hope back to her room where she could get some rest.

Faith put Hope back into her bed and then the three girls started to clean up the mess from the art supplies. They couldn't help but notice that Hope had fallen asleep, so they wrote a little note telling her they enjoyed the day, and they would see her soon. Faith quietly placed the note beside Hope's bed and then they left.

The following week was very busy, but the girls went back as much as they could to spend time with Hope. She seemed to be doing well, but on December 19th while Faith was volunteering, she stopped in Hope's room and found out that Hope had taken a turn for the worse. Her little friend was lying motionless. Hope's parents Billy and Brenda were sitting by their daughter's bed with their heads hanging low and tears running down their faces.

"What happened?" Faith heard herself cry out.

"Oh Faith," said Brenda sobbing. "She has a bad infection that's causing a high fever. She was struggling to breathe, so they had to sedate her and put her on a ventilator. You know with complications like this it could take her life."

"No! I don't accept that!" Faith exclaimed, as she paced back and forth. "We're not going to lose her. We have to believe and trust that God is in control and He will restore health to her. He will perform a miracle. He can and He will!!"

"Yes, we want to believe that," said Billy. "But it's hard, it's just so hard."

Faith knelt down between them, grabbed their hands, and proceeded to witness to them both. She told them that they needed to pray and trust God to move this mountain in their lives. She told them of how her parents had to trust and believe for her and now they had to trust and believe for their daughter. She asked them to join her by laying their hands on Hope and praying together for God's healing, strength, and mercy. They did as she asked, and Faith led them in prayer.

"Lord, we come to you and ask that you would heal Hope. Lord, you know her, you created her, and Lord I know and believe you can heal her completely. This situation, this illness, is a mountain before this family; a mountain that seems too big to climb, but Lord your word says in Matthew 21:21-22 that we can speak to the mountains and they will move. Lord we speak to this mountain with faith and not doubting. Show us your miracle healing power. Give Billy and Brenda the strength they need to stand on your word and believe that you can do this that we ask. Heal Hope Lord, we ask this in Jesus ' name. Amen."

When Faith finished praying, she hugged Billy and Brenda. She gave Brenda her phone number and asked her to please call her if there was any change in Hope's condition. Before she left to continue her shift she again expressed to them that God was faithful and that He can heal.

She told them that she was going to get ahold of her church and have Hope put on the prayer chain. Many people would be praying and believing for Hope's healing.

"I for one believe that Hope will be in my Sunday school class one day soon," said Faith. "God will make a way, you'll see."

Billy and Brenda thanked Faith for praying and for taking Hope under her wing and being such a great friend to their little girl; they said Hope was blessed to have her. With a smile on her face and her hand upon her heart Faith said to them that she was the blessed one to have Hope in her life. With that being said Faith turned and walked out of the room.

A few days had passed and there was no change in Hope's condition. Faith, Denise, and Marcie sat with Billy and Brenda as often as they possibly could. It was hard to believe that Christmas was almost there; the days were going by fast.

Determined to provide some comfort and support to Billy and Brenda, Faith and the girls made arrangements to bring food to the hospital on Christmas Eve. They planned to sit together, pray, and believe God for a miracle healing and that's exactly what they did. They stayed at the hospital until about nine o'clock in the evening but then had to leave because church service was at ten o'clock the next morning. Emotionally exhausted the girls drove to their homes and went straight to bed.

Morning came quickly and it was time to get ready for church, Christmas Day had arrived. Faith got up and looked at her phone to see if she had missed a call. No calls and no messages, she felt her heart sink a bit. Gazing out the window and breathing in she gathered her thoughts and focused her mind on God. Again, she found herself praying for her little friend in the hospital. Her thoughts were interrupted when she heard her parents yell, "Merry Christmas Faith."

"Merry Christmas," she yelled back.

A couple minutes later her parents came to her room to get a hug. "We love you baby," they said.

"I love you guys too."

"What's wrong sweetie?" Mom asked, as she noticed the disturbed look on her daughter's face. "Are you thinking about Hope?"

"Yes, I can't help it. I'm just so sad that God hasn't moved yet. I know He can heal her."

"Don't give up baby, keep believing."

"Yes, it's Christmas," said Dad, "we will believe for a Christmas miracle!"

"Sounds great Dad, I do believe!"

"Alright then, let's get ready and go to service," he said with a smile, as he walked out of the room.

The Braydans got ready and headed to church. Christmas music filled the car as they drove and the fresh fallen snow made a blanket of white on the ground. It was absolutely beautiful. Just witnessing the beauty of God's creation stirred up a feeling of hope. It inspired a strong sense of believing. As they entered the church, people all around were greeting each other and expressing wishes for a Merry Christmas. The love being shared amongst the people was palpable and just so lovely. Service was about to start so the Braydans quickly made their way to their seats.

Pastor Dan stood up, welcomed everyone, wished all a Merry Christmas, opened in prayer, and invited everyone to give their best praise and worship to the Lord. The music began and worship service was truly anointed. You could feel the Lord's presence as the voices sang out and the sounds of the instruments filled the air. God was surely present and amongst His people. It was a celebration of our Lord and Savior.

After worship was over Pastor Dan proceeded to give the message. As he spoke, he talked about Christ's birth and how we needed a Savior to come in the manner in which he came. He was born in the humblest of beginnings and walked in a way only He could. Christ experienced human problems and emotions just as we do in order to show us that He truly understands what we go through and how we feel.

He was not a king on a throne with everything handed to Him; He was not born with the proverbial silver spoon in His mouth as earthly kings are. He was born with a purpose that only He could fulfill. He was going to later die on the cross and make a way for us to have everlasting life. We could call on Him in our times of trouble; He could provide peace, healing, deliverance, and more. But first we had to ask Him to forgive us of our sins and we had to accept Him as our Lord and Savior. We had to believe that He is the Son of God that was born for us, died for us, and rose again! He is our greatest gift from God and we needed to give thanks and praise to Him.

Faith was hanging on every word that was being spoken when all of a sudden her phone started to vibrate. She quickly pulled it out of her purse and seen that there was a text message from Brenda. Pausing for just a moment she closed her eyes, took a breath, and then started to read the message, *Hope is off the ventilator and breathing great on her own; she's sitting up in bed! Her temperature is gone and she is doing great. They can't explain it, but all her symptoms are gone. It's a Christmas Miracle! Faith we got our Christmas Miracle!!* Faith started crying as she read the message. Dr. and Mrs. Braydan quietly leaned over and asked if she was ok.

Without saying a word, she handed them the phone and let them read it for themselves. In an instant she found herself standing and raising her hand up to get Pastor Dan's attention. As he looked over to Faith he asked, "Faith is everything okay?"

"Yes Pastor Dan!" she said with excitement. "I'm sorry for interrupting but I just got a text message about Hope, the little girl at the hospital that we've all been praying for and well, she's up and doing great. She received the healing we've all been praying for. It's a Christmas Miracle!! I just had to tell everyone and Praise God like you said to."

"Praise God!" said Pastor Dan. "Thank you all for praying for Hope. What a great gift for us to receive this day, news of her healing." The crowd erupted in praise to God. Pastor Dan turned toward the worship team and with a motion of his hand they knew to start playing and singing again. After some time was spent in heartfelt worship Pastor Dan concluded the service with a prayer and church was dismissed. We all left service that day with a joyful heart knowing God truly hears our prayers and He is faithful to us; what a wonderful gift!

Faith's Locket

Chapter 10

A couple of weeks have passed since the exciting news of Hopes healing. Billy, Brenda, and Hope are planning on coming to church Sunday. Faith is thrilled to have them come as her special guests and she is overjoyed that Hope will be in her class. She, Denise and Marcie have been very busy planning a special celebration for Hope that will take place during class time. The girls have been praising God non-stop for His faithfulness in hearing their prayers and healing their little friend.

Faith looked at her watch and noticed it was almost time for class to start. The kids were getting settled in and playing with some toys while they waited for Hope to arrive. Within a few minutes Billy, Brenda, and Hope were at the door.

Hope was a bit nervous to come into class because she had never been there before and she didn't know any of the other children, but when she arrived in the classroom a little boy named Jasper made her feel very welcome. He ran up to her with a toy in his hand, reached it to her, and said come on let's play. His smile radiated pure joy and his enthusiasm was contagious. Before you knew it Jasper's cousin Mia was standing right beside them with a box of donut holes in her hand and offering them a treat. Billy and Brenda were standing off to the side watching Hope's interaction with the kids. When they saw that Hope was going to be fine and that she was actually enjoying being there they waved to Faith and headed toward the sanctuary. Faith smiled, waved back, and then closed the door.

When Billy and Brenda reached the sanctuary the Braydan's noticed them walking in. Dr. Braydan got up from his seat, welcomed them, and asked if they would like to join him and Mrs. Braydan. Happy to see a familiar face they graciously accepted and sat down beside them.

Pastor Dan began to speak from Luke 15:11-24 about the prodigal son. He told how this man had two sons and how the one son wanted to leave his father's house. The son no longer wanted to live the life he was raised to live. He no longer wanted to follow the rules his father had set in place for him. The lifestyle he was brought up in no longer appealed to him. This young man wanted to choose his own path. He wanted his inheritance from his father and he chose to take what he had coming to him and he left. What fun he thought he was going to have, living his life, his way with no restrictions, no guidelines, and no expectations on his behavior. No accountability, he could come and go as he pleased. Well, this young man found out that his so-called good times only lasted as long as the money did. He soon realized what and who he turned his back on. He had a father that loved him and only wanted good things for him, but he chose to turn his back on his father and walk away. Now he was alone, homeless, hungry, and dirty. Life couldn't get much worse as he contemplated eating with the pigs. He thought to himself that maybe he could go back home and be a hired hand at his father's place. Would his father forgive him, he wondered? He knew his father had every right to be angry and choose not to forgive him, but he had to chance it, so he started on his journey back home to ask for forgiveness. When his father saw him coming from a ways off he started rejoicing that his son had come back home. His father forgave him because he loved him. His father gave him the best robe he had; he got a ring for his hand and shoes for his feet. This earthly father rejoiced at the returning of his lost son and showered him with love. But even as much as our earthly father can love us, our heavenly father loves us more. (Matthew 7:11) speaks of "how even those being evil know how to give good gifts unto their children but how much more our Father in heaven will give good things to them that ask him."

Our heavenly father waits with open arms for the lost to call out to him and ask him for forgiveness. (1 John 1:9) says "if we confess our sins, he is faithful and just to forgive us our sins, and to cleanse us from all unrighteousness." (Revelations 3:20-22) says "Behold, I stand at the door, and knock: if any man hears my voice, and opens the door, I will come in to him, and will sup with him, and he with me. 21 To him that overcometh will I grant to sit with me in my throne, even as I overcame, and am set down with my Father in his throne. 22 He that hath an ear let him hear what the Spirit saith unto the churches."

As Pastor Danny was speaking Billy couldn't help but feel the presence of the Holy Spirit knocking on his heart, he could hardly sit still in his seat. It was as if the Pastor was speaking directly to him. His heart raced as thoughts of what his life was like when he used to live for the Lord played in his mind. He, like the prodigal son, chose to turn his back on the Lord and on his upbringing. His wife and child were not raised in the ways of the Lord as he was, so they didn't realize anything was missing from their life. They had never experienced the love of the Lord, that is until they met Faith. She showed them through her actions, through her compassion, and through her words, that God was real and that He loved them. Because of Faith's witnessing and God's healing Hope, they were all touched by His Love and they were at church today.

As Pastor Danny continued giving the message he said, "There's a place for you in God's family. There's a place for you right here in this church, all are welcome. God's waiting for you to come unto Him. You can accept Him into your heart right now and join the family of Christ. The altar is open if you would like to come pray."

Just about that time the students and teachers from the Sunday school classes entered the sanctuary. Faith and Hope walked over and sat down with Billy, Brenda, and the Braydans. Faith was glowing as she got to have her new friends visit her church. Hope finally got to be in her class and it blessed her to see this family come to the house of the Lord. How she longed in her heart for them to find their way to the Lord.

Before closing the service, Pastor Danny noticed this new family sitting with the Braydans. When he saw the little girl, he figured it had to be Hope so he asked Faith if this was indeed Hope and her parents. Faith stood up with the biggest smile on her face, hand rose in praise and said, "Yes!!" He then asked Faith to please bring her friends down front and introduce them to the congregation. With that being said the six of them headed toward the altar. Faith excitedly did the introductions. Pastor Danny turned to Billy and asked if there was anything he would like to say.

Billy humbly said, "Yes, I would like that." He started by saying, "I just wanted to thank everyone for praying when Hope was in the hospital. We know that it was your prayers that God honored. He gave us strength through a very trying time and He performed a healing that only He could perform. Faith had told us that her church was praying, and we could feel the love and prayers from everyone, even though we only knew the Braydans, Marcie and Denise. When we arrived here today, we were greeted with much love." He paused for a moment with tears starting to well up in his eyes; he looked at Brenda and Hope. Brenda gazed back at him with tears rolling down her cheek and they spoke to each other without saying a word, as married couples sometimes do. With a nod of Brenda's head and a smile on her face Billy knew she confirmed that they both felt God calling them to be a part of His family and this church.

Turning toward the Pastor he continued to say, "We feel God's presence here and we would love to be a part of this church; we want to give our hearts to the Lord and live for Him." Praise you Jesus was being shouted by everyone. Pastor Danny immediately called for everyone to gather up front to pray with this new family. With the anointing of oil and the laying on of hands the congregation joined in praying with Billy, Brenda, and Hope as they accepted Jesus as their Lord and Savior. The Holy Spirit filled that place with a palpable love as these three gave themselves to God.

Faith's Locket

Chapter 11

It's hard to believe that six months have already passed by; summer is upon us and the Braydans are planning a well-deserved trip. They started packing last week but something always seems to come up and interrupt the process. Their rooms are messy, but they don't mind because they are excited and looking forward to going on an adventure. They've discussed many times how important it is to spend special times together and how they never want to take those times for granted. Time is fleeting and they know how crucial it is to enjoy each other's company whenever you get a chance to. Working in the medical field is a constant reminder of how precious life really is. The Braydans live with the knowledge that no one is promised tomorrow, so they believe we all must live life with no regrets. We should always take time to show one another just how valuable each other are and to lift someone up if at all possible. Life is like a vapor, here today, and gone tomorrow.

It's Saturday evening and the Braydans are back at it again, trying to finish packing for Hawaii, when all of a sudden the phone rings. "I got it," yells Dr. Braydan. "Hello, yes this is he. Ok we'll be right there."

"What is it?" asked Betty.

"There's been an accident and a young girl is en route to the hospital. She's in bad shape and they need us to meet in the OR."

Without hesitation Dr. Braydan and Nurse Betty quickly got ready to leave. They stopped by Faith's room and explained what has happened. Faith asks if she should go with them. They told her no and that she should stay home and continue packing. They hugged her good-bye, told her they loved her, and then were out the door.

The Braydans arrived at the hospital just before the ambulance got there. They scrubbed in and within moments they were performing surgery. The young girl had been injured in a Sea Doo accident. Apparently, she was going too fast and she didn't notice the large boulders that were just beneath the water's surface. Her Sea Doo hit one boulder causing her to be ejected off her craft as she was thrust forcibly into the water, she unfortunately landed on to another boulder causing her to sustain serious injuries. The Braydans and the rest of the OR team worked diligently and performed the lifesaving procedures she needed.

After the surgery was completed and the young girl was moved into recovery, the Braydans went into the waiting room to give her parents an update. When they approached the entrance, a couple came rushing toward them with an intense look of worry on their faces.

"How is she, is she okay?" they asked.

"Yes, she's going to be fine," Dr. Braydan answered. "Let's sit for a moment and we'll explain everything."

As they sat, they talked about the injuries she sustained and also about the recovery period and therapy that she would need. The girl's parents could hardly stop crying and they kept thanking the Braydans for all they had done for their daughter.

Nurse Betty grabbed the mother's hand and said, "It was our pleasure. We also have a daughter about the same age and if she needed help, we would want someone to do all they could to help her."

After they finished talking, they walked the parents to the recovery area so they could be with their daughter. When the Braydans finished filling out some paperwork it was time to head back home. Once they were situated in the car, they called Faith.

"Hello," said Faith, as she answered the phone.

"Hey sweetie, just wanted to let you know we are on our way home and that everything went well. We'll pick up a snack on the way and then do some more packing after we eat."

"Ok sounds great guys; I could use a snack," she giggles. "See you soon."

"Ok baby, we love you."

"Love you guys too."

Faith kept packing as she waited for her parents to get home. While driving the Braydans discussed how glad they were to be able to help the young girl that had the accident. They couldn't imagine seeing Faith in a situation like that; it would be devastating to them. They talked about how blessed and how truly happy they were to have Faith in their life. This trip they had coming up was going to be so much fun. The three of them spending quality time together was something they all needed.

Faith was lost in thought dreaming about the perfect vacation as she placed items into her suitcase, when all of a sudden, the doorbell rang. "Coming," she yells, as she runs down the stairs to unlock the door. "I'm glad you're here," she said, as she turned the knob. "I'm hungry!"

When the door was fully opened, she looked up and said, "Oh hi Sheriff Glenn, I'm sorry I thought you were my parents," she chuckled. "They're not here right now, but they are on their way. Would you like to come in?"

"Faith," he said, as he stepped inside, "I'm afraid I have some bad news."

"Bad news? What is it? Is my Grandma ok? Questions were flowing out of her. Her mind raced as she wondered what Sheriff Glenn was going to say. She stared at his face anticipating his answer, but she said, "Maybe you should wait until Mom and Dad get here and you can tell us all together. They should be pulling up any moment."

Sheriff Glenn looked at Faith with his eyes full of compassion. "Listen to me Faith," he said, as he stepped closer to her. "What I need to say is very difficult. It's about your parents. They were killed in a car accident."

"No, you must be mistaken!" she yelled out. "I just talked to them a little while ago. I'm telling you they'll be here any minute."

"I'm so sorry Faith," he continued, and in that moment, she started to fall. He reached out and caught her. He gracefully eased her down to the floor and cradled her in his arms as she wept.

The word of the accident spread quickly. Grandma Martha was notified by the authorities and she immediately headed to the house to be with Faith. Denise and Marcie were at the hospital working when they heard the news. They instantly asked their supervisor if it was okay to leave to go be with their dear friend. She immediately gave them permission to go, so they took off running down the hospital hallway. As they approached the elevator, they saw Danny, Brandon, and Nicole waiting there for the doors to open. None of them could believe that such a tragedy had happened, but one thing for sure they all knew it was of the utmost importance to get to their friend. When the elevator door opened, they got in, pressed the down button, and they were on their way. They quickly got to the first floor, made their way to their cars, and headed to Faith's house.

Grandma Martha arrived at the house and found Sheriff Glenn on the floor holding Faith in his arms. She sat down beside them and took Faith into her arms. They sobbed as they couldn't believe this happened. Within a few minutes Faith's friends arrived and ran through the door; they all fell to the floor and wrapped their arms around Faith and her Grandma. At that moment no one could speak; they were overcome with sadness and disbelief. After a while had passed the group coaxed Faith to get up and sit on the couch in the living room. Once everyone calmed down, Faith asked the Sheriff what exactly happened. He proceeded to say that a man in a large truck had hit them head on and they were killed instantly; they didn't suffer.

"I still don't understand," said Faith, in between sobs. "Why did he hit them? What happened? What caused him to hit them?

"We are investigating that, and we will let you know as soon as we have some answers." Nothing he could say would bring reason or comfort. Her heart was broken; her life shattered in a million pieces.

"Again, I'm sorry," he said. "I'll excuse myself for now and get back to the precinct. Please don't hesitate to call us if you need anything," he hugged Faith and Grandma Martha, then he left.

Grandma Martha and the group of friends decided to stay with Faith. None of them were going to leave her alone; they were in for the long haul. Denise and Marcie sat on the couch beside her and held her tightly. Nicole asked Faith if she could get her a drink. Faith shook her head no, but Nicole went to the kitchen anyways and brought her back a glass of water. The others went with Grandma Martha upstairs to get some pillows and blankets because they knew it was going to be a long night. They sat around for hours sometimes chatting softly and other times sitting in complete silence, but they were together and that's what mattered most. After some time had passed, they were able to get Faith to eat a little bit. They decided to turn on the TV just to have a little distraction. Emotionally exhausted, they all ended up falling asleep right there in the living room.

Morning came and Grandma Martha was the first to wake. She went into the kitchen to start the coffee. Nicole heard her and immediately followed. Nicole told Grandma to please go and sit down that she would take care of making the coffee and breakfast. She quickly gathered things from the pantry and fridge; before you knew it the coffee was done and she had a large spread of food ready. Nicole poured Grandma a cup of coffee and made her a plate of food.

"Here you go Grandma," she said, with a smile on her face.

"Thank you so much Nicole, this is very sweet of you. Thank you for being such a good friend to my granddaughter."

"You're very welcome. What else can I do? I want to help in any way I can."

"Well, today's going to be very difficult. Faith and I have to go to the funeral home and get the funeral arrangements started. I know my son had prepaid and made their final arrangements, but there are always last-minute things that have to be taken care of. I'm sure Denise and Marcie will want to go with Faith and me to handle those things, so if you could stay at the house and be here to answer calls and such that would be a great help."

"You can count on me. I'll be here."

"Thank you sweetie," said Grandma Martha.

It wasn't long and you could hear footsteps in the living room, as the others were starting to get up. Before long everyone made their way to the kitchen. Morning greetings and hugs were going on all around. Coffee was being poured and plates of food made. Faith even poured a glass of juice, grabbed a pancake, and started nibbling on it.

"Thank you all for being here with me," said Faith. "I couldn't get through this without you."

"You're welcome," they said collectively, as they sat down around the table.

Looking at Grandma, Faith asked what needed to be done. Grandma told her they would have quite a bit of running around to do and that Denise and Marcie could go with them. She also said that Nicole was going to stay around the house and take care of anything that came up there. Danny and Brandon were going to fill in wherever needed; first thing to take care of was notifying the airlines and hotel that the trip needed to be cancelled. They all planned to regather at the house later in the day and spend the night there again. After they finished eating, everyone got ready to conquer the tasks of the day.

Grandma, Faith, Denise, and Marcie got changed and headed out to handle the funeral arrangements. Danny and Brandon headed to the travel agency in order to make sure the trip was cancelled correctly. After everyone was out of the house, Nicole cleaned up the breakfast mess and then loaded some food in a slow cooker so there would be something to eat later when everyone gathered back in. As she walked around the house she was overcome with sadness for her friend, her heart started to race. She wanted to do everything possible to ease any burden.

When she walked past Faith's room, she looked in and saw the partially packed suitcase and clothes strewn all over Faith's bed. This image crushed her, and she could only imagine how Faith was going to feel when she had to look at it, let alone when she would have to unpack. Nicole didn't want Faith to have to go through that, so she decided to unpack the suitcase and put away all of Faith's clothes. The phone rang like crazy, but she was able to finish cleaning up the room in between calls.

Dr. and Nurse Braydan's room was cluttered in the same way as Faith's with partially packed luggage and clothes spread on the bed; but Nicole couldn't bring herself to go into their room so instead she pulled the door shut and headed down the stairs. Just as she was about to go check on the food the front doorbell rang. She opened the door to find the Braydan's dear friend Sharon standing there with tears streaming down her face. Nicole embraced her and asked her to come inside. Sharon has known the Braydan's since high school. She stood up in their wedding and is Faith's Godmother. Once inside and calmed down, Nicole filled her in on what everyone was doing.

The Braydans had asked Sharon many years ago that in the event of their death could she personally handle some things for them. She agreed and knew their wishes. She came to the house to be there for Faith and to let her and Grandma Martha know that she was going to take care of reserving the hall and planning the funeral luncheon. Sharon owns the local radio station in town WJOY, and she would notify the community through her broadcast about the tragic loss of these two wonderful people. She could relay all the funeral information on air in lieu of making so many phone calls. She would however have to make some out-of-town phone calls to friends and family that need to be notified. Everything was set in motion and people were stepping up and helping as they could, but it didn't make the loss any more bearable. The community was shaken, and we all knew it was going to take some time to recover.

Faith's Locket

Karen Young

Chapter 12

Four days have passed since the tragic event that took two pillars of our community. The day was upon us when we would all gather together and pay our last respects to these wonderful people. The Braydans would be missed terribly. Grandma Martha and friends have not left Faith's side. They have stayed at the house every day and night since the accident. The mood in the house is very somber. The funeral service is scheduled to start in just a couple hours. Denise and Marcie are helping Faith get dressed while the others are waiting downstairs in the living room. Danny and Brandon have already lined the cars up in the circular drive near the front door so it will be easier for everyone to get in. All of a sudden the sound of footsteps filled the quiet of the house. Everyone that was waiting in the living room stood up knowing that Faith was about to come down the stairs and enter the room. After hugs and a prayer, they all got into the cars and headed toward the church.

The drive was quiet, no one saying a word. The day was gray and gloomy as if the earth itself was in mourning. As they drove through town you couldn't help but notice the love the community had for the Braydans as there were signs and flowers lining the sidewalks for many blocks; even the light posts had bouquets of flowers tied to them. When they arrived at the church there were people standing outside because there was no more available space indoors. Danny and Brandon pulled up and parked the cars right next to the church entrance. Everyone got out of the cars and quickly gathered around Faith and Grandma Martha, then they walked into the church together. As they made their way down the center aisle everyone in the church stood up. The caskets were up front, and the Pastor was standing there waiting to greet Faith. Once Faith and her friends were seated the service was to begin.

The pews up front were filled with family and closest friends. Co-workers sat side by side filling many of the seats. The love and support that surrounded Faith was one of the most heartfelt sites you could imagine. Faith stared at the caskets as she put her hand up toward her neck, grabbed the locket, and started rubbing it between her fingers. Pastor Dan spoke so compassionately; it was one of the most touching funeral services I had ever attended. There wasn't a dry eye in the sanctuary as everyone undeniable felt how great this loss was. The most beautiful songs were sung and story after story was shared of how the Braydans had touched the lives of so many people. After the service was over a private luncheon for the family and close friends was to take place. Sharon had it all arranged as she followed the Braydan's instructions exactly according to their wishes. It was absolutely gorgeous.

The luncheon had been going on for a couple hours when Faith went over to Sharon and thanked her for all the work she did. Emotionally exhausted, Faith wanted to go home. Sharon told her that she should go on and not worry about anything else; she had it all taken care of. Faith hugged her good-bye and told her she loved her. Grandma and friends came up behind them and told Sharon she did a great job. They also let her know they were going home with Faith, so not to worry they would still be with her. "Thank you," she said, as she hugged them all good-bye.

The drive home was very emotional; Faith cried softly while Denise and Marcie did their best to provide comfort to their friend. Danny was driving the car they were in and Brandon was following close behind with Grandma Martha and Nicole. The sense of finality was so strong and overpowering; the heartbreak was almost unbearable.

As they pulled into the driveway Faith looked up, took a deep breath, and prepared to go into the house. Once everyone was inside Faith turned to Grandma and her friends and said, "Thank you guys so much for being with me through all of this, but I'm so tired; if you don't mind, I'd like to go lie down."

"You're welcome, go get some rest," they said, as each of them hugged her before she started up the stairs.

"Would you like me to bring you some water or anything else?" asked Denise.

"No thank you," she said, as she turned and started to ascend the staircase.

The group looked at each other with sadness in their eyes. As Faith passed by her parent's room the door was shut, she looked at it and wiped the tips of her fingers across it as she continued toward her own room. When she got to her room she plopped down on her bed without even changing her clothes. She grabbed the blanket that was lying across the foot of the bed, wrapped up in it, and was fast asleep within a few minutes.

"Do you think she's ok?" asked Danny. "I haven't heard her moving around at all up there."

"I'm sure she's fine," said Grandma.

"Marcie and I will go check on her. We'll be really quiet and peek in." said Denise.

The two of them almost silently walked up the stairs. When they approached her room, they looked inside and seen she was sound asleep. They walked quietly to the bedside and adjusted the blanket. Before leaving the room, they turned on the night light that was on Faith's dresser. Without making a sound they exited the room and pulled the door slightly shut behind them. When they got back downstairs, they told everyone she was asleep. The rest of the group devoid of energy as well decided it was time to get some rest. They all settled in and ended up sleeping right where they landed, some on the living room furniture and some on the floor.

Morning came and the sounds of the birds chirping outside Faith's window woke her up. She opened her eyes, pushed off the blanket, and made her way to the window. She stood there and gazed at the morning sun glistening on the water. She knew life would never be the same, but it was time to start working toward a bit of normalcy. Hearing some noises coming from downstairs she knew that some of the others were awake. She cleaned herself up and got dressed for the day. When she got to the kitchen, everyone was sitting around the table.

"Good morning," they said collectively.

"Good morning," she replied.

"Would you like some breakfast?" asked Nicole. "Sit down and I'll get it for you."

"Ok thanks Nicole, but just a little and some orange juice." Faith joined the others at the table while Nicole prepared her breakfast.

"I wanted to thank you all again for everything you've done for me but it's time for things to get somewhat back too normal. You don't have to put your lives on hold anymore and stay with me around the clock. I'll be fine."

"I'm not leaving you alone yet," said Denise, as she grabbed Faith's hand. "You're at least stuck with me."

"That's right me too," said Marcie, as she grabbed Faith's other hand.

"Ok, well you two can stay, but seriously I know the rest of you have to get back to work and you're not going to function well if you don't take care of yourselves. The rest of you guys should get back into your normal routines. I love you all so much and you have things you need to do; I understand and I'll be ok."

"If that's what you want Faith we will do that," said Grandma. "But I will be coming in and out often. I'm going to be around a lot."

Looking at Grandma with a loving smile she says, "That's good Grandma I wouldn't expect anything less from you."

"If you're sure you don't need us we will do what you want," said Nicole. Danny and Brandon nodded in agreement.

"I'm sure and you guys can come over and visit whenever you want."

Everyone gave into with what Faith wanted. When breakfast was over they cleaned up the mess and the ones leaving started gathering their things. Within about an hour Grandma, Danny, Brandon, and Nicole had their things packed up and ready to go.

"Ok sweetie," said Grandma, reaching toward Faith for a hug, "I guess we're going to leave now, but if you need anything you better call me."

"Or call any of us," the others chimed in.

"I will I promise, but I'll be fine," she said, with a slight smile.

After they hugged each other good-bye they left. Faith, Denise, and Marcie decided that they still needed a day of rest, so they plopped down on the couch with the pillows and blankets and started a movie.

Chapter 13

About a week has passed since the funeral and the girls are still staying with Faith. The parent's room remains untouched and door closed. Denise and Marcie know that it's going to be hard on Faith to box up her parent's things, so they decide it's time to offer their help and see if she's ready to start that task.

Saturday morning as they were sitting at the breakfast table Denise looked at Marcie and they knew it was time to ask; Denise starts by saying, "Faith we know this is going to be difficult, but Marcie and I think it would be good if we helped you clean and box up your parent's things."

Faith's heart started to pound a little faster, tears started welling up in her eyes, but she knew her friends were right, so she nodded in agreement.

"We'll go at whatever pace you need us to," said Marcie. "You can tell us what you want to keep, if you want to donate, and where to donate. We will make sure everything is done exactly how you want it."

"I appreciate that," replied Faith, as she wiped a tear off her own cheek. "I know there's no way I could do this on my own."

"Well there's no way we would let you," said the girls.

Denise got up and said, "Well we need boxes so I'm going to run out and get some; I'll be back in a bit. Do you need me to pick up anything else while I'm out? Would you like a smoothie?"

"That would be nice," the girls replied.

"Ok, see you when I get back."

After Denise left, Marcie and Faith started cleaning up the kitchen. Faith's heart was heavy. She dreaded the thought of getting rid of her parent's things, but she knew it had to be done. Life would never be the same, but it couldn't stop. She had to push herself to move forward; life has to go on. When the kitchen was done, she and Marcie went out on the deck to wait for Denise to get back. They settled into the lawn chairs and breathed in the fresh air. The warmth of the sun felt nice and the sound of the birds was very pleasant. The water sparkled and the boats sailed smoothly by. It wasn't long and they could hear Denise hollering that she was back, so they got up and went inside the house.

"Here are your drinks," said Denise, as she handed them to the girls.

"Thanks," they said, as they reached out to receive them.

Denise said she'd be right back as she headed out to the car.

"Do you need help?" asked Marcie.

"No, I got it."

Within a couple minutes Denise returned and placed the boxes at the foot of the stairs. "Ready when you guys are. I'm pretty sure I got enough, but if we need more I'll go back out and get them."

"I'm ready," said Faith, as she grabbed a couple boxes and started up the stairs.

Denise and Marcie grabbed some as well and followed her. When Faith got to her parent's room she paused for a moment, took a deep breath, looked at her friends, and turned the doorknob. When the door opened, she saw the partially packed suitcases and clothes that were meant for the trip lying on the bed; she sighed heavily. Denise and Marcie put their boxes down and placed their arms around Faith, "You can do this," they said. "We got you." With that being said they entered the room.

"How would you like us to sort the clothes?" asked Denise.

"Honestly I'm not sure how to go about this," said Faith, with a look of distress on her face.

"Ok, no worries we'll go slowly; let's first take care of the clothes that are already out. You look as we fold and tell us what box to put them in; donate to church, keep, or donate to poor."

"Sounds good," replied Faith, as she sat on the bed and gently brushed her hand across some of the clothes.

Denise and Marcie started picking up the clothes and folding them as Faith instructed what box they should go in. After all the clothes were cleared off the bed they decided to continue by doing one drawer at a time. When the boxes got filled the girls carried them out of the room and stacked them in the hallway. As they continued working, Faith came across some of her parent's favorite sweatshirts. She lifted them close to her face and breathed them in. Just holding the shirts brought her a feeling of being close to them. She turned to her friends and said, "Keep these," as she handed the shirts to them. They smiled, gently folded the shirts, and piled them neatly on the bed to keep.

Drawer after drawer were emptied. When they were finished with the dressers they moved on to the closets. At this time, they were only boxing up clothing and shoes; the personal items such as jewelry and keepsakes would wait for another day. They knew if they could get through all of the clothes that would be an incredible accomplishment. There was no need to put Faith through too much in one day. The girls made great progress; within about 5 hours they had all of the clothes separated, boxed up, and labeled as to where they should be taken.

By this time, the girls were exhausted both emotionally and physically. They decided to leave the boxes stacked in the upstairs hallway. It was definitely time to quit for the evening and it was also time to get something for dinner; they decided to order pizza. Denise grabbed the phone and placed the order. She was not really thinking clearly and ended up ordering way too much food, so they invited Danny, Brandon, and Nicole to come by. The girls cleaned themselves up, changed their clothes, and then waited for their friends and the food to show up.

Danny, Brandon, and Nicole got to the house before the food arrived. As the friends were gathered in the living room talking, the doorbell rang. Danny and Brandon quickly went to the door and paid for the pizza.

"Hey, we invited you for dinner," said Denise. "You're not supposed to pay for it!"

"Don't you worry about it," they said, with a smile. "Let's eat!"

The crew went to the kitchen, got plates and supplies ready, poured drinks, prayed, and started eating. The company was just what the girls needed. The day had been taxing to say the least. Some good food and laughter was just what they needed to lift their spirits.

After dinner was over they played some games. It felt good to relax and enjoy one another's company. As they played one game after another their conversation got around to what they had been doing that day. Denise jumped in and told them about how they packed up Faith's parents' clothes. Faith's countenance dropped a bit.

"I'm sorry you had to go through that Faith, but it's really good you guys got so much done," said Nicole.

"It really is good," the boys chimed in. "What did you do with all the boxes?"

"They're upstairs in the hallway," answered Faith. "All labeled and ready to be delivered to the church or the shelter, but we were too tired to do anymore."

The boys told her not to worry about carrying the boxes down the stairs or about delivering them to the proper locations. They would borrow a truck from a friend of theirs, come back tomorrow, load them up, and drop them off where they belonged. The girls couldn't thank them enough. That was a huge burden lifted off their shoulders. They breathed a sigh of relief knowing the boys were taking care of that.

"Having friends rally behind you, especially in a time such as this, really is such a wonderful blessing," said Faith. "I can't express to you all how much you mean to me."

The friends gathered around Faith and gave her a group hug. "We love you Faith," they said collectively. Then they sat back down and started playing another game.

Laughter filled the house that evening. It was a sound Faith wasn't sure would ever take place there again, but she was so happy it did. The bible says in (Ecclesiastes 3:4) "there is a time to weep, and a time to laugh; a time to mourn, and a time to dance;" thankfully this moment was a time to laugh.

Chapter 14

Faith is moving forward, going on with what is now her new normal. The girls have been moved out for several weeks and Faith finds herself sometimes in a big empty house. She is staying busy with her schooling, volunteer responsibilities, and also with her Sunday school obligations. Her friends and Grandma Martha make it a point to check in on her and visit as often as possible. Her church family has also made sure to reach out with calls, cards, or just a simple note to let her know she's not alone. But with everyone going back to their own schedules, it does make it a bit more difficult to get together as often as they would like.

Somedays Faith finds it a bit difficult to go to the hospital just for the sheer fact that she's used to seeing her parents walking in the halls. When she feels sadness trying to overtake her, she pauses for a moment, closes her eyes, and pictures her parents with smiles on their faces doing what they loved to do, helping people. This vision encourages Faith to continue on and provide help in any way she can.

The CEO of the hospital has asked for Faith to please stop by his office today at two o'clock; she can't imagine why he would want to see her. When she arrived at his office, he politely asked for her to come in and have a seat.

"Would you like something to drink?" He asks.

"No thank you, I'm fine."

He proceeded to explain to her why he asked her to come in. "Faith, your parents were a huge part of this community and an even bigger part of this hospital and it was our privilege to have had them work here for so many years. We want to honor them by dedicating the new Cardiac Unit in their name, The Braydan Cardiac Unit. They poured their heart and soul into this place and into their patients. We couldn't imagine opening the unit under any other name."

Faith was overjoyed. She couldn't believe that such an honor was being bestowed upon her parents, in their memory. "Thank you so much," she said, as she stood up and hugged him. "My parents would be so excited and yet so humbled at the same time to receive such an honor."

"They deserve it," he replied. "There will be a ribbon cutting ceremony in a few weeks and the hospital staff would love it if you would be there to cut the ribbon. You can invite anyone you want to attend, and we will have refreshments afterwards."

"It would be my pleasure," she said, as she placed her hand on her heart. "I'll tell my Grandma and some of our church family so they can attend. Thanks again for this special recognition," she said, as she reached out, shook his hand, and then left.

Faith worked that day with a bit more zeal than she had in sometime. This news picked her spirits up to a higher level. She could hardly wait for her shift to be over so she could call Grandma

Martha and of course she wanted to go to the cemetery and tell her parents. She knew they really couldn't hear her speaking to them, but it was just something that made her feel better.

As she continued on with her day, she saw Denise and Marcie by the fourth-floor nurses' station. She walked over to them at such a quick pace she was almost running. She shared the news of the new unit dedication with them and they couldn't have been prouder.

"This calls for celebration," Denise said.

They all agreed, and a celebration get together was in the works. In Braydan style they decided to go to Outback and celebrate. Dr. Braydan loved going there and he had many times taken the group of friends there to celebrate a special occasion. Faith sent out a group text and invited Grandma Martha, Danny, Brandon and Nicole. Response texts came in quickly and everyone was available, so Faith called Outback and made the reservations.

The girls still had a couple hours to work, so they hugged each other and said they would meet up at the restaurant at six o'clock. Excited to have impromptu plans, the girls walked away with enthusiasm. Faith was very elated just thinking about the great honor her parents were to receive and she was also so pleased that her friends could all come to dinner and celebrate with her.

As she walked away and headed to Room 254, she found herself humming a song, something she hasn't done since her parent's passed. It felt good she thought to herself. Arriving at the entrance of the room she said hello as she always does and then started to approach the bed. To her surprise it was Henry. "Hi Henry," she said.

"Hi Faith," he replied, with the biggest smile he could give.

"How have you been Henry? It's so good to see you, but I hope it's nothing serious. What brings you back into the hospital?"

"Nothing bad, just a little congestion, but you know with us old folks they don't take any chances. I was hoping to see you while I was in here. You are such a sweet girl Faith; you made my last visit here bearable."

"Awe thanks Henry, that's nice of you to say. So what can I do for you this time?"

"How about another adventure?" he said, with a slight smirk on his face.

"Ok, I'll be right back. You know the drill; I have to go get permission."

She took off whistling a tune because she was pretty sure the nurses would give her the go ahead. "All aboard," she said, as she entered the room with the wheelchair.

Henry smiled at her as he tried to get out of bed on his own.

"Oh no you don't!" said Faith. "Let me help you so you don't fall."

In no time Faith had Henry perfectly secured in the wheelchair and they were on their way. The sun was shining brightly through the windows and you could see the rays of sunlight penetrating through the air; what a gorgeous site! They had great conversation as they journeyed through the halls. Faith shared the news about her parents. Henry was very sad to hear of their passing. He apologized for not reaching out to her and for not coming to the funeral, but he didn't know about the accident. Faith assured him that it was ok. She then changed the conversation to the news about the new cardiac unit. Henry asked if she would take him by there so he could see it, so she did. Henry thought it was a lovely gesture on the part of the hospital to dedicate it to her parents. She whole heartily agreed. It was a beautiful addition to an already amazing facility.

Faith glanced down at her watch and noticed that her shift was almost over. "Well Henry looks like I need to take you back to your room. My shift is ending and I'm meeting my Grandma and some friends for dinner."

"Sounds good; thanks again for showing such kindness to me and for taking me on another stroll."

"It was my pleasure."

A few more twists and turns down the halls and they would be back at Henry's room. "Here we are Henry, back safe and sound."

Faith carefully assisted Henry back into the bed. Once he was all tucked in, she got him a glass of water, placed it on his tray, and told him good-bye. She paused at the doorway, looked back, and smiled. "It was really great seeing you again Henry. Have a good night," she said, as she waved and walked out.

Faith found herself once again humming a joyful tune. She really enjoyed her visit with Henry and now she was going to have fun with her friends and Grandma. First, she had to stop at her locker and put some things away. Then, she needed to grab her purse and she'd be ready to go. This was a great day she thought to herself. She exited the hospital, looked up, smiled, and said, "Thank you Lord for a great day."

Faith's Locket

Chapter 15

The dedication ceremony was beautiful, and The Braydan Cardiac Unit is now up and running. It's hard to believe that the ceremony took place 2 months ago. Faith has been going through the motions of life, but some days have been harder than others. She stops by the cemetery often and when she really wants to feel close to her parents, she puts on one of their sweatshirts and talks out loud to them. When she talks to her mom she usually sits or lies on her parent's bed, but when the talk is directed to her dad she finds herself curled up in a ball in his favorite chair. While this action temporarily helps her get through a difficult moment, it is definitely not fulfilling to her spirit; she misses her parents terribly. As the days go by the feeling of loneliness grows; the gaping hole in her heart gets bigger and bigger. The grief is more than she can bear. Of course her Grandma and her friends are still a huge part of her life and they are with her as much as possible, but it doesn't fill the emptiness in the house or in her heart. Her parents meant everything to Faith and in the quiet evenings at home, the devil gets in her ear and whispers words of discouragement as only he can.

Going to school and work is becoming more and more difficult. Daily tasks are like hurtles she has to jump over, and they feel as though they get bigger by the day. She wonders how much more she can take.

One day while at the hospital, Faith was going about her usual routine checking in on patients and seeing if there was anything she could do for them. When she walked into Room 420 she glanced at the white board hanging on the wall and noticed a familiar name. Her heart started pounding extremely fast; she quickly looked at the patient and realized it was the man that caused the accident that took the lives of her parents. This was more than she could handle. She ran out of the room crying. As she ran down the hallway, she almost knocked Denise over. Denise tried to stop her, but Faith kept running. Denise wondered what possibly could've happened, so she checked the name of the patient in the room Faith ran out of. She immediately realized who it was and knew exactly what was going on. Scared for her friend, she quickly called Grandma Martha and explained what had happened. Grandma dropped what she was doing and headed to the house. She figured Faith would be headed home and she wanted to get there as fast as she could so Faith wouldn't be alone. Denise went to Michelle and told her what happened, and that Faith had left. She asked if she could get off work early to go be with Faith, but they were short staffed that day and the hospital couldn't let her go. The only thing she could do was say a quick prayer.

When Grandma Martha arrived at the house and walked up to the front door, she noticed it wasn't completely closed. She gently pushed it open and walked inside. She called out to Faith, but there was no response. Grandma walked around the main level looking to see if Faith was anywhere down there. She peeked out on to the patio and didn't see her there either. Grandma walked back toward the front of the house and she then heard crying; it was coming from upstairs. Grandma went up and found Faith lying on her parent's bed. She walked over to the bed, sat down, and put her arms around Faith trying to comfort her.

"Faith sweetie," she said, "I know what happened and I'm so sorry you had to face that. I'm here for you honey, you're not alone."

Faith abruptly pushed Grandma's arm away and stood up. "Of course I'm alone! Do you see my parents here? This room is empty just like this locket is empty!" Faith ripped her locket off her neck and threw it in her mom's empty dresser drawer. "Mom and Dad said I would know exactly what to put in this locket, that it would be something precious to my heart, but my heart is broken and I have no use for this locket. I can't look at it let alone wear it without it being a constant reminder of this huge loss.

"Why did God take them? I needed them and the people in this community needed them. How can I believe in a God that would let such a horrible thing happen? Oh, and the drunk that caused the accident still lives…how is that fair?"

"Honey I understand the hurt you're feeling, but you know sometimes things happen that make no sense. We will never understand why they were taken from us in this way, but I do know that God loves us and did not forsake us. He is with us right now. He has a plan and even though we don't know what that plan is we must trust in Him."

"I'm not sure I can believe that anymore. It sure doesn't feel like He's here or that He cares; and a plan…what kind of plan?" Faith cried out, as she walked out of the room.

Grandma followed Faith and tried to talk more to her, but she didn't want any part of it. There was nothing she could say to make her feel better. Grandma told Faith she was going to stay the night, but Faith didn't care. She told Grandma to do whatever she wanted to do. Faith went to her room and shut the door. Grandma gently touched the outside of the door, told Faith she loved her, and then headed downstairs.

Faith's sadness was turning into anger and bitterness and unfortunately it was growing at a rapid pace. Denise and Marcie both texted Faith and asked if they could come over, but Faith told them no; she was going to bed and turning her phone off. They then texted Grandma Martha to make sure Faith was going to be ok. They let her know they tried to come over, but Faith didn't want them to. Grandma told them not to worry; she was going to stay over. She also told them Faith was going to need their patience and prayers, even if it was from a distance for a while. The girls couldn't help but feel helpless, but they considered what Grandma said and decided to give Faith a little space.

Faith took a leave of absence from work and she rarely showed up at school. Word spread quickly about what happened and that Faith was struggling. Friends rallied, people sent messages and cards, but she ignored them for the most part. She quit going to church and her Sunday school kids were missing her terribly. Jasper, Mia, and Hope sent cards and pictures they colored, but she was spiraling out of control and nothing seemed to ground her.

One day while Faith was at home the doorbell rang. She went to answer it only to find a single red rose with a note attached to it lying on the welcome mat. She bent down, picked it up, and read the message: *Trust in the Lord with all thine heart; and lean not unto thine own understanding. In all thy ways acknowledge Him, and He shall direct thy paths. (Proverbs 3:5-6)* "Yea right," she said, as she brought the rose into the house and tossed it on the sofa table in the living room. She went about her day going in and out of the house, from the deck to the couch, back out to the deck again. She couldn't find any peace. Frustrated with everything she decided to go to bed. Maybe tomorrow would be a better day.

Morning came and Faith made her way down to the kitchen. She poured herself a glass of orange juice and went out to the deck. To her surprise lay another rose and another note. This one was on her lounge chair. She picked it up and started reading the note: *Peace I leave with you, my peace I give unto you: not as the world giveth, give I unto you. Let not your heart be troubled, neither let it be afraid. (John 14:27)* She looked around and saw no one. She placed the rose on the table next to her chair, as she drifted off in thought. When she went back into the house, she placed this rose by the other one.

The phone rang; Faith looked at it, took a breath and answered, "Hey Denise, what's up?"

"Hi, I miss you," she said. "Would you like to go out to lunch?"

"No, I'm really not up to it. I think I'm just going to hang out here today and rest. Hey Denise, you haven't been to my house in the last couple days have you?"

"You know I haven't Faith, why would you ask me that?"

"Never mind it's nothing. I got to go," she said, as she hung up the phone.

A couple days later Faith decided to go to the cemetery. She grabbed a bottle of water and headed out the door. The weather was nice, but she didn't seem to notice. When Faith got to the cemetery she walked up to the graves, spread out a blanket, and sat down. She picked at the blades of grass and didn't say a word. When her eyes glanced up at the writing on the headstone's tears rolled down her cheeks and a feeling of heartbreak washed over her again. "I'll never be the same again," she said, as she stood up and started folding the blanket; then she turned and walked toward her car.

As she approached her car, she noticed a rose stuck on her windshield. How is this possible she thought, as she looked around and there were no other cars in sight? She didn't see anyone else in the cemetery either. Just like the other roses this one had a note as well: *He healeth the broken in heart, and bindeth up their wounds. (Psalm 147:3)* "Hello," she said, as she looked around. "Is anyone out there?" Not seeing anyone she got in her car and drove home. She carried the rose and note into the house and place it with the others. Confused and tired she went to lie down.

The next morning Grandma Martha came over, used her key, and walked in. She hollered out to Faith, but there was no answer. She walked by the sofa table and saw the roses there, she touched them as she walked by, but she didn't read the notes. Grandma went to the patio door and saw Faith out on the deck. She slid the door opened and said, "Hey sweetie, how are you today?"

"I'm ok Grandma," she replied. "Hey Grandma, have you been sending me roses and notes?"

"No sweetie, I haven't. Are you talking about the ones on the sofa table?"

"Yes, it's so weird. I keep finding these roses in random places and I can't figure out who is sending them. There's no name on the cards."

"Really, that's interesting. I'm sure you'll find out eventually."

"Yea I guess so. It's just strange because the messages sound so familiar. I mean it's just scripture and I'm familiar with the scriptures, but that's not what I mean; it's weird because it's like they are talking to me and they arrive at the right time when I need a specific word."

"So, do you believe in God again; do you trust Him again?"

"That's not what I'm saying Grandma. I'm just saying it's odd. What purpose could these flowers and notes serve?"

"Everything has a purpose, and everybody has a purpose. You have a purpose Faith. For one thing your Sunday school kids are missing you; they want their teacher back."

Grandma continued witnessing to Faith, explaining to her that her friends and church family all miss her. She told her she has a calling that only she can fulfill. Grandma reminded Faith that her parents raised her to believe in God and they would be so sad to know that she is wavering in her faith. She reminded her about the paper she wrote in class regarding how and why her parents picked the name Faith and how much they believed. They didn't doubt when an obstacle got in their way; they knew God would move it if they believed in Him.

Faith assured Grandma that she knew all those things and remembered them, but she wasn't ready to trust God. Grandma let Faith know that God was still there waiting with open arms; He didn't leave her or forsake her, and she would be praying that Faith would have an open heart and find her way back to Jesus.

Grandma asked Faith if she would like for her to stay and spend the night, but Faith told her no; she was fine to be there by herself. Grandma said she understood, but could they at least go out and get something to eat or order food in.

Faith agreed that going out to lunch would be nice, so they got ready and headed to the restaurant. They each took their own cars so that after lunch they could go their separate ways. Grandma was ok with that because she needed to go on some visitations at the local nursing home. While they were eating, Faith looked out the restaurant window at the Bay and couldn't help but notice a beautiful sailboat with a huge cross on its sail. As it floated by, she noticed a scripture reference on the back, Hebrews 11:6. It seemed like God was surrounding her everywhere she went trying to get her attention. She jotted down the scripture reference in her notes and planned on looking it up when she got home.

When they were done eating, Faith thanked her Grandma for taking her out to lunch. They hugged each other good-bye and went on their own way.

Faith's mind was preoccupied as she drove home pondering what the verse was from the back of the sailboat. When she arrived home, she drove up the circle drive, got out of the car, and found yet another rose; this one was tied to the front door knocker. She carefully untied it and went into the house. She walked into the living room and sat down, rose in hand wondering what was going on. She proceeded to look at the card, once again it was scriptures and no name. This one said: *Verily I say unto you, if ye have faith, and doubt not, ye shall not only do this which is done to the fig tree, but also if ye shall say unto this mountain, Be thou removed, and be thou cast into the sea; it shall be done. And all things, whatsoever ye shall ask in prayer, believing, ye shall receive.* (Matthew 21:21-22)

For we walk by faith, not by sight. (II Corinthians 5:7) Now *faith is the substance of things hoped for, the evidence of things not seen.* (Hebrews 11:1) These she knew well. The love she felt from these notes started to crack the hard exterior shell that she was allowing to form around her heart. The walls that were erected were being penetrated by the love that was exuding in these messages.

As she sat on the couch, tears streamed down her face. How is this possible she thought; who is writing these? Her mind flashed back to the sailboat; what was that scripture she thought. She grabbed her dad's Bible and opened it up. She flipped through the pages until she reached the verse: "But without faith it is impossible to please Him; for he that cometh to God must believe that He is, and that He is a rewarder of them that diligently seek Him." (Hebrews 11:6)

Faith reached over and grabbed the blanket that was hanging on the back of the couch. She scooted her body down until her head rested on the pillow and then covered herself up. She clutched her dad's Bible tightly in her arms and dozed off to sleep.

Morning came and Faith found herself still on the couch; she had slept there all night. She got up and went upstairs to take a shower. As she was drying her hair, she heard a knock at the door. She quickly ran down the stairs yelling, "I'm coming, hold on a minute," but when she got to the door there was once again no one there; however, there was a rose. She bent down and picked up the flower, but to her surprise there was a stamp on the back of the card with the florist name on it. This is it, she thought; finally, I'll be able to find out who's sending these flowers. She finished getting ready and drove to the florist. Excited to get some information she quickly got out of her car, walked into the florist, and approached the desk.

"Hi Cheryl," she said to the clerk.

"Oh hi Faith, how are you?"

"Well that all depends. I have a question for you. For about a week now I've been receiving flowers at random places with a note attached, but no name identifying the sender or the florist until this morning I received one that had your florist name stamped on the back. I was wondering if you could tell me who sent it."

"I'm really not supposed to give out that kind of information," said Cheryl.

"No, you have to tell me," Faith started crying. "I have to know."

Cheryl hesitated but felt sorry for Faith, so she cooperated with her request and started looking through the files. "Ok I think I have it. What did the card say?"

Faith grabbed the card and started to read it: *For I know the plans I have for you, declares the Lord, plans to prosper you and not to harm you, plans to give you hope and a future. (Jeremiah 29:11)*

"Ok I got it. It was ordered by Sharon."

"Really, are you sure?"

"Yep, I'm positive!"

"Thank you so much Cheryl," said Faith, as she quickly exited the store.

Faith immediately got into her car, called Sharon, and asked if she could stop by. Sharon was happy to hear from Faith and told her yes, please, come over; she'd love to see her. Faith's heart was pounding; she wasn't sure how to feel. Why was Sharon sending her flowers with notes and no name? Her mind whirled with possible scenarios playing out in her head. When Faith arrived at Sharon's house, she grabbed the last rose, walked up to the door, and knocked. Sharon answered the door and immediately saw the rose; she knew right then what the visit was about.

"Hi sweetie," she said, as she reached for a hug.

"Sharon what's going on?" asked Faith. "Why are you sending me flowers and not signing the cards?"

"I'm not Faith," she answered.

"I know it was you, this last one had the florist name on it, and I made them tell me who sent it. Why would you lie to me?"

Sharon asked Faith to come in so she could explain what was going on. She asked her to please sit down, that there was quite a bit she had to tell her. As she began to speak her voice got a bit shaky. "Ok, it's like this…you know your mom and dad were my best friends. They asked me many years ago that if they passed, would I follow through with their last wishes. Of course I told them I would do anything for them, but never in my mind did I ever think I would have to fulfill those wishes. I always thought one day when we were old and gray, we would burn the envelope they gave me without ever having to open it; unfortunately, that didn't happen. When they passed, I had to sit down and read their last requests. Sweetie, you were their world and they wanted everything done a certain way and they wanted you to be taken care of."

Faith got up and started to pace the floor. She took a deep breath, as her eyes welled up with tears.

"Sweetie, are you ok; do you want me to keep telling you about this?"

"Yes," said Faith, as she sat back down.

"Ok," she said, as she grabbed Faith's hand. "I have done my best to follow their instructions to the exact detail. They told me that you would probably come by seeking answers and when you did, I was supposed to give you an envelope that was addressed to you." Sharon got up at that moment and went over to a box where the letter lay waiting to be delivered to Faith. "Here you go sweetie, I'll give you some privacy so you can read it." Sharon walked out of the room. Faith rubbed the envelope so gently; she slowly opened it and started reading:

Our Dear Daughter Faith,

We sit and write this letter hoping it will not have to be used, but if it does then its ok. Know in your heart that we are fine and you will be too. We know you must be hurting, but Honey never lose hope. Keep the faith in your heart that you've always had. You are and always have been our very special blessing.

We asked Sharon that in the event of our untimely death, would she please follow our precise instructions as we knew you would be hurting. We told her to keep a very close watch on you, but to do it from a distance so you wouldn't notice. We told her that when she saw you hit a low point, if you started to spiral, to please do these things that we ask. We filled out notes that were to be attached to a single red rose and delivered to you at specific locations when the situation arose. If you're reading this letter, it means that she has done exactly what we asked.

Honey, it's ok to grieve, but only for a short while. Don't let grief consume you. Don't let it deter your path or let it derail you from your calling. Sweetie, it's time to let the peace of God that only He can give, to rest upon you. We love you so much and are so proud of you. Pick yourself up and be the light we know you are. We will see you again someday and we'll have the best reunion. But for now, LIVE!! Live life to the fullest, for we know what an amazing gift life is. Walk in God's ways and let Him use you as He sees fit.

Now give Sharon a hug and let her know we thank her for doing such a great job; we knew we could count on her.

We love you both.
We will always be with you, watching over you.
We love you forever and always,
Dad and Mom

Faith was amazed at the forethought her parents had in writing the letter. Laying out such specific loving wishes to provide comfort to her made her hardened heart melt. Love is the most precious gift one can give or receive and for that love to be demonstrated in such a way was more touching than she ever could've imagined. The love from her parents and the love from Jesus encompassed her. She knew it was time to start living again, laying all bitterness and resentment aside. She hugged and thanked Sharon as her parents asked her to in the letter, but she couldn't stay because there was something else she had to do.

Chapter 16

Faith was leaving Sharon's house that day with a new outlook on life. She had a letter from her parents that she would treasure forever; not to mention all the roses and notes that touched her more than she ever thought possible. She got in her car that day with life breathed into her by the Holy Spirit through the words He led her parents to write down many years ago. The Word of God accomplishes what it needs to in the perfect timing that God has for it.

As soon as Faith got to her house, she unlocked the door and immediately ran up the stairs and went into her parent's room. She opened her mom's dresser drawer and retrieved her locket. Her hands shook with excitement as she put her locket back on. She rubbed it between her fingers and smiled; it felt so good to be wearing it again.

Faith couldn't wait to tell Grandma Martha and her friends what had happened. She had been so closed off, not really talking to any of them and she felt bad. It was time to get things back on track. She wanted to tell them all at the same time, so she planned an impromptu game night. Grabbing her phone, she typed out a group text message: *Hey guys I'm sorry I've been distant please forgive me. I was wondering if you were available to come over tonight at 6pm for some pizza and game night. There's something important I want to tell you all. Text me back and let me know if you can make it. Love you all, Faith.*

Instantly responses started flying in; her phone was buzzing like crazy. Everyone was excited and coming. Nothing could keep them away. Faith went around the house making sure everything was organized and ready for her company to come over. She got the games out and stacked them on the kitchen counter. She also got out the plates, cups, and other party supplies they would need. When she was finished setting things up she paused, looked around, and smiled. She went out onto the deck, raised her hands towards the sky, and Praised the Lord, thanking Him for His faithfulness, then said I love you mom and dad. After a few moments of taking in the beauty God had created, she went back into the house to finish getting ready for her guests.

It wasn't long before the guests started to arrive. With each guest's arrival the level of excitement went up a notch. The friends had missed each other very much and were so happy to be together again. Grandma Martha was overjoyed to see the smile on her granddaughter's face that had been missing for some time. After the last guest arrived, Faith asked them all to gather together in the living room; it was time to share what had been going on.

Faith began by thanking her friends for always being there for her. Even when she blocked them out of her life, she knew in her heart they were only a phone call away. She started explaining how she had reached the lowest point in her life and wasn't sure how or if she was going to survive. As she continued talking, she walked over to the sofa table and picked up the roses to show them to the group. She went on to explain how the roses and notes started showing up and how they spoke so loudly to her heart. Not knowing where they came from or who sent them was unsettling, but with the last flower sent, she got a clue. She followed the clue and it led her on a journey of discovery and healing. The group was hanging on every word. You could hear a pin drop it was so quiet. Faith proceeded by reading every card and telling them where she was when it arrived. As she continued telling everyone what happened, she pulled out the letter from her parents and read it to them. There wasn't a dry eye in the room as everyone undeniably felt the love within the words of that letter. When she was done reading, they all gathered around Faith and hugged her. They thanked her for sharing such a personal and beautiful experience with them and they expressed how good it was to have her back. While they stood there rejoicing, the doorbell rang. The pizza had arrived. Danny and Brandon once again beat Faith to the door and paid for the pizza. The group made their way to the kitchen and the party was started.

The next morning Faith went back to work with a renewed zeal to serve her fellow man. Love and forgiveness filled her heart. She walked into the hospital and greeted everyone she saw with a big smile on her face. She made her way through the hospital and checked in at the nurse's station on the 4th floor. When she looked at the patient manifest, she noticed the man that caused her parent's accident was still in the hospital. She knew exactly what she had to do. In a few moments, she found herself walking toward his room. As she arrived at his room, she walked in and said, "Hello my name is Faith. I just wanted to say I'm so sorry for running out of your room the way I did."

The man looked up in amazement. "I know who you are and I'm the one that's sorry. How is it possible that you would come into my room and apologize to me?"

"Well, it's the right thing to do. It has taken me quite a while to get to this point, but it's what God would want me to do. He wants me to forgive you and I believe my parents would want me to do that also."

"I don't understand how you could ever forgive me," he replied.

"That's what the Christian walk is all about. If we let Jesus be our Lord and Savior by asking Him into our hearts, He is just to forgive us all our sins. He set the example for us to follow. He forgives us and we must also forgive others."

"You mean to tell me that Jesus would forgive me?"

"Yes, He absolutely would, you just have to pray and ask Him," she answered.

"I would like that very much. Would you help me pray?"

"I would love to."

In that moment, Faith grabbed the man's hands. Tears of forgiveness, tears of healing, flowed down both their faces as she led Him in the sinner's prayer. A man she thought at one point she would hate forever, was now becoming a brother in Christ. It was a moment she will never forget. There was no better thing she could've done that day. After they finished praying she said, "Welcome to the family of Christ." She smiled and told him she had to go check on some other patients, but she didn't want to leave without asking if he needed anything else. He smiled back at her and told her no; she had given him more than he ever imagined. She poured a glass of water for him, sat it on his tray, gave a little wave, and left.

The rest of her day went splendidly. It felt so good to be back at work doing what she knew was one of her callings. The hours passed quickly, and it was time to go home. She took a moment and walked by the Braydan Cardiac Unit; pausing at the entrance she touched the brass plaque that hung on the wall, displaying a picture of her parents along with their names engraved upon it. She smiled and said, "I'm back Mom and Dad; I hope to always make you as proud of me as I am of you, I love you." After that she made her way to her locker, gathered her things, and went home for the evening.

Tomorrow was Sunday and Faith was overjoyed as she planned to go back to church. She wanted to get a lesson prepared for her class and she also wanted to make some special treats for them. She missed the kids and was looking forward to seeing them. Faith went to the kitchen to start making up treat bags when her phone rang; it was a three-way call from Denise and Marcie. They asked what she was up to, so she let them in on her surprise.

"Well you know we're not going to let you have all the fun, we're coming over to help," they said.

"Ok," said Faith. "See you in a few," as she hung up the phone and continued getting supplies ready.

Within about 30 minutes, Denise and Marcie was at the door with a carryout from the local burger joint. Faith answered the door

Faith's Locket

and was happy they had picked up food. She was so excited to get home and start on the kid's stuff that she had forgotten to get anything for dinner. After the girls ate, they started making cookies. They laid out the treats in piles to be bagged up. As soon as the cookies were cooled, they wrapped them individually so they could be safely added to the treat bags. Cookies, toys, and art supplies were placed in each one. After the treats were assembled, they helped Faith put together an art project for the kids to do in class. When they had completed all the stuff for Sunday school, they decided to kick back and watch a movie. The girls decided to spend the night, so they once again found themselves hunkered down with pillows and blankets in the living room.

Morning seemed to come quickly, and the girls were up getting ready for church. They gathered the packages, and they were soon on their way. When they arrived at church, the people were thrilled to see Faith. The girls could hardly make it through the halls of the church because everyone wanted to talk to Faith and let her know they were so glad to see her. Faith thanked everyone for their kind words, but she really needed to get to class to set things up. She barely got things organized before the kids started to arrive. Jasper was the first one. He was walking in the hallway with his mom and dad when he got a glimpse of Faith standing in the entrance of the room. He took off running towards her yelling her name. When he got to her, he hugged her and wouldn't let go. The other children did the same thing. Faith was on her knees surrounded by the kids, none of them willing to let her go.

Chapter 17

Fall is upon us once again and the colors are brilliant and breathtakingly beautiful. Faith takes time out every morning as she focuses on God before going about her day, praying that He leads and guides her in every step she takes. She walks throughout her day now with a renewed joy in her heart, knowing what a special gift life really is. Classes are going amazingly well and her work at the hospital and the church are keeping her very busy. Her schedule doesn't allow for much free time, but she doesn't mind because she loves what she does. Faith and her friends hang out as much as they possibly can, even if it's just for a quick lunch in the hospital cafeteria.

One day when Faith was doing her rounds, she saw a bunch of her friends hanging out at the 5th floor nurses' station, so she stopped by to say hi. The group was talking about how some of their patients had told them they had received a special gift from an unknown sender. While the gifts were not all the same, they did have one thing in common. For example, one gift might be a golf magazine for a person interested in golf, or a needlepoint kit for someone that does needlepoint, but the common thing was that a mustard seed was glued on it with a message saying, *God Loves You.* The group stood there trying to figure out who could possibly be giving out these special gifts.

"It must be a new hire," said Denise.

"Probably so, since it just started happening," said Danny.

"Well, it has to be someone that has access to every floor," said Nicole. "Because I've been all over the hospital the past few days and have heard stories from patients on every floor."

"It could be anyone," said Brandon. "So many different positions have access to all the floors. For instance, Rad techs like Danny and I have to go all over the hospital when we do portables, then there are transporters, food servers, janitorial; the list is too big to be able to figure it out."

The friends all agreed that while it was interesting and nice, they would probably never know who it was. They decided to call the person "The Mustard Seed Angel" since that was the only common denominator within the gifts. As much fun as it was to stand around and speculate who it could be, they had to get back to work, so they said bye to each other and went on their separate ways.

Faith walked around the counter and grabbed the patient manifest as she looked it over she saw that Room 523 was her next stop. A big smile came upon her face because she recognized the patient's name. It was a 12-year-old boy from her church. She walked in and blurted out, "Hello Holston, what in the world did you do?"

"Oh hi Faith, I broke my leg playing hockey, but it doesn't hurt as bad as it looks."

"Well, I'm here to see if I can get you anything?" she asked.

"Can I have a coke?"

"Absolutely, I'll go get you one."

"Can you visit with me for a while?"

"I can't right now, but I can come back after my shift is over."

"That would be awesome, we can play cards. Someone left me a deck of cards in my room. I went for an x-ray and when I came back there was a brand-new deck of hockey-themed cards on my tray."

"Sounds great, I'll beat you at some rummy," she laughed.

Faith walked out of the room and then returned with a coke for Holston. She sat it on his tray and told him she'd be back in a little while. Room by room, patient by patient, she went about helping in any way she could. When she finished with her shift, she stopped by the cafeteria and picked up some snacks to take to Holston's room. Since he was in for a broken leg, there weren't any dietary restrictions she had to worry about, so she knew it would be ok to bring some munchies to snack on while they played cards.

"You ready to lose?" Faith joked, as she walked into the room.

"Oh right, I'm pretty sure I'll win," said Holston. "It's really cool someone left these cards for me. I don't know who did it, and I have no idea why there's a seed glued on the box."

"Yea it's a mustard seed. My friends were talking about how all sorts of random gifts have been showing up in patient's rooms. They nicknamed the person The Mustard Seed Angel."

"That's awesome," replied Holston.

"Ok, hand me the cards and I'll start shuffling."

Faith dealt out the cards and the game began. They laughed and joked as they played each hand. Sometimes Holston was scoring more points, but then the next hand Faith would catch up.

They bantered back and forth about who was going to win. When it was Holston's turn to deal, Faith got up and put some snacks into a bowl; she also had brought him another pop, but this one was caffeine free.

"Hey, what happened? Isn't there any more coke?" he laughed.

"Yea right, like I'm going to load you up with a ton of caffeine this late. Remember I work here, and the nurses are my friends. The last thing they want on the night shift is a hyper preteen!"

They both cracked up as they thought about it. Faith played for a little while longer, but she knew it was time to leave because visiting hours were just about over. Of course she could've gotten away with staying later because she works there, but she didn't want to set a bad example by disobeying the rules. Faith cleaned up the snack mess and Holston put the cards back into the box. He thanked Faith for spending time with him and for all the snacks she brought. She told him she had a great time and if she has a chance she'll try to come by another night and play some more. When she left his room, she pulled the door slightly closed so Holston could watch hockey on TV without disturbing any of the other rooms nearby.

Faith was walking down the hallway when her phone started to vibrate; it was a text from Denise and Marcie. *Hey, what are you doing? We tried calling earlier and you didn't answer. We're going to grab a bite to eat at the Oven and then go bowl a couple games; do you want to come?*

Faith responded, *Absolutely, I'm starving! Sorry I missed your call; my phone was on vibrate and it was in my purse. Holston from church is in the hospital with a broken leg, so I stopped by his room and played rummy with him. But yes, I'm coming; order me a burger and fries. I'll be right there.*

Faith quickly made her way through the hospital and out to her car. Luckily the restaurant wasn't far away, so she knew there'd be no problem getting there before the food arrived at the table. She was so excited to have a spontaneous night out with the girls. Shortly after she walked into the restaurant, Cindy approached the table and asked her what she would like to drink. The water was fine, Faith told her, and in a couple minutes the food was there. The girls talked about how fast the year seemed to be going by. They could hardly believe Thanksgiving was coming up; it would be here before they knew it. Faith asked the girls if they would be available to come to her house for Thanksgiving dinner. She was planning on getting the whole crew together if possible. Grandma Martha already said she would love to come for dinner, but she had plans to go for dessert at her friend's house, which works out perfectly because Faith was planning some games for after dinner that the younger crowd would enjoy, but Grandma wouldn't know how to play. Denise and Marcie told Faith they wouldn't miss it. Denise's parents were going out of town to be with her dad's parents for the holiday and Marcie's parents were invited to a friend's house. Everything was coming together nicely; now all she had to do was check with Danny, Brandon, and Nicole.

The girls finished their food and headed to the bowling alley. While they were standing at the bowling alley counter paying for their lane, they heard some voices yelling for them. When they turned around, surprisingly enough, Danny, Brandon, and Nicole were running toward them.

"Oh my goodness you guys, funny bumping into you here; we were just talking about you," said Faith.

"Really, what about?" asked Nicole.

Faith filled them in on the Thanksgiving plans and asked if they could make it. They were all available and accepted the invitation with excitement. They asked the girls if they would like to join them on the lanes they were at. Of course they wanted to, so Danny went up to the counter and asked the cashier if she would please add them to their lanes and cancel the ones they were scheduled to go on. The spontaneous evening turned out to be super entertaining; crazy pictures were being taken left and right, definitely a night to remember.

Chapter 18

A couple weeks have gone by and the Mustard Seed Angel gifts have been turning up everywhere. Whoever was behind this gift giving has been very busy, not to mention very secretive. No one has a clue as to their identity. The patient's morale has been very uplifted by this act of kindness shown to them. Those who received a gift have expressed that they wish they knew who it was so they could say thank you. Denise came up with an idea to take a Polaroid picture of every patient holding the gift they received and then they could write a thank you note on the picture. She would then collect all the pictures and display them on a bulletin board in the hospital. The patients were thrilled to have this opportunity to say thank you. The spirit of gratitude was palpable within the walls of the hospital; with Thanksgiving just a few days away, it was perfect.

On Monday, Faith was excitedly walking through the halls humming a little tune as her mind kept drifting off to thoughts of her upcoming dinner. As soon as her shift was over she was going to the grocery store to pick up the last items she needed. She could hardly contain herself and time just couldn't go by quickly enough. Denise and Marcie caught up with her in the hallway and asked her if there was anything they could do to help with the dinner. She told them that she had everything under control, and she was picking up a few last-minute items as soon as she got off work, but if they really wanted to help they could come by early on Thanksgiving Day. They happily agreed and said they would be there by nine in the morning with some breakfast sandwiches. They also offered to go to the grocery store with her that evening, but they both still had a couple hours left on their shift. Faith thanked them but said she could barely wait for the last fifteen minutes of her shift to get over let alone wait another two hours; she was just too excited. She would be fine going by herself and she would see them tomorrow at work. Denise warned her to be careful that it was starting to sleet outside. Faith assured her that she would be and off she went. Marcie and Denise looked at each other and smiled; they were both so happy that their friend was so full of joy.

Faith made one last stop checking on a patient in Room 223; as soon as she was done she headed to her locker. She quickly gathered her things and hurried to her car.

When Faith got in, she paused for a moment and turned on the radio; a big smile came across her face as she was thrilled that it was finally time to go to the store. After she finished shopping, she got back in the car and texted Denise and Marcie, letting them know she was safe and heading home. Denise and Marcie both received the text and thanked her for letting them know she was okay, and they would see her tomorrow.

Meanwhile, at the hospital Denise and Marcie were finishing up their shifts. Since they were both working until six o'clock, they decided to go out to dinner together after work. They planned on meeting near the emergency exit so they could walk out to their cars together. When they arrived in emergency, an ambulance was pulling in, so they stood off to the side to give the paramedics a clear pathway. They looked on as the EMTs pushed the gurney into the ER. A cold chill went up their spine and their legs got weak as they saw it was Faith lying on the gurney. They ran up to the EMTs and started asking questions, but they were unable to stop and answer. The EMTs pushed their way through the swinging doors and the girls were left standing there wondering what had happened. They immediately made their way to the emergency waiting room. Denise called Grandma Martha and Marcie started sending out texts. Danny, Brandon, and Nicole showed up almost instantly because they were still at the hospital working; Grandma was about fifteen minutes away. When the group saw Grandma walk in, they all ran to her side and hugged her.

"What happened?" asked Grandma, as she looked around frantically.

"We're not sure," the girls answered. "We were just about to head out for the evening when an ambulance pulled up, so we stepped aside to let them by and to our shock Faith was on the gurney. Now that you're here we can go up to the desk and ask questions."

With that being said Grandma rushed up to the desk and started asking for information. The nurse told her she would go and check on Faith's status and be right back. Grandma started to sway a bit, so Danny and Brandon each held an arm and assisted her in sitting down. The group sat there anxiously waiting to hear something. About twenty minutes later the nurse showed back up and said Faith was in a coma. She was scheduled for a lot of tests, so it would be quite some time before they knew anything else. According to the EMTs she apparently must've lost control of her car, slid off the road, and ending up hitting a tree.

Grandma broke down and started to cry uncontrollably. The whole group had tears streaming down their faces, but they tried to maintain a sense of composure for Grandma's sake. They had to be strong for her and for Faith. Denise took out her phone and started making calls; first call was to Pastor Danny. He told her he'd be right there, but before heading over he called Billy and Brenda and told them to get a prayer chain going. Denise also called Sharon to let her know what happened and of course Sharon started crying and said she'd be right over. Before long, Pastor Danny, Sharon, and Grandma Martha's friends Jay and Hannah all showed up in the ER.

As the group sat there feeling helpless, the minutes felt as though they were going in reverse; time was moving slower than ever before. Waiting to hear news about Faith's condition was unbearable. The thought of another tragic loss was something none of them could handle. They had to believe that Faith would be okay. Everyone grabbed hands right there in the waiting room and started crying out to God to please touch her and make her well. They would all stand in the gap for Faith and not waver in their belief that God was able to heal her and not only able to, but that He would do it.

Night was falling and they found themselves hunkered down in the waiting room not willing to leave for a moment. Finally, about three o'clock in the morning one of the nurses approached the group and said she was still in a coma, but they had her settled into a room in the ICU. They could all go to that waiting room and then take turns, two people at a time to visit by her bed side. They quickly gathered their things and headed up to the ICU. Grandma Martha and Pastor Danny were going in first; then the rest of them would take turns.

Walking into the room and seeing Faith hooked up to all the lifesaving machines was devastating. Even though most of them were used to seeing it on a daily basis, it affected them differently because it was Faith. After everyone took a turn going in, Grandma Martha told Jay and Hannah she appreciated them coming, but that they should go home and get some rest. They could pray from home just as easily as praying from the waiting room. They complied with her request and started to leave, but first they made her promise to call if she needed anything. Grandma assured them she would be fine because none of Faith's friends were budging; they were staying until Faith woke up, so she wouldn't be alone.

Pastor Danny decided to have a special prayer meeting take place at the church for Faith at nine o'clock that Tuesday morning. He sent the message out through the prayer group and also asked Sharon to announce it on her radio station. That way, everyone would have a chance to hear about it and be able to gather together and pray for Faith's healing; anyone that wanted to come was welcome. When the time came, the church was almost filled to capacity. The love that was being poured out for Faith was absolutely beautiful. Sharon also decided to have a candlelight vigil every evening at six o'clock on the hospital grounds right below Faith's window, so she announced that as well. They would sing a few worship songs and pray there every night.

Grandma Martha, Denise, Marcie, and the rest of the crew got to stay in Faith's room. The Doctors decided that it might help if they stayed in there and talked to her; maybe hearing their voices would help Faith to fight and wake up. They all took turns talking about different things, reminiscing of fun times in the past. Denise thought it would be a good idea to read the note cards that the Braydan's had written out for the roses, so she went to the house and got them. She was headed back to the hospital to read them to Faith, but it was like her car was driving itself and she found herself in front of the florist. She looked over in amazement and knew she was supposed to bring back some roses, so she picked up a few dozen and headed back to the hospital. She knew the Braydans would want Faith to have roses in her room. When she got back, she set up the vases of flowers; one on the windowsill, one on the tray by the bed, and the other on the table at the foot of the bed. When she finished, she stood next to Faith and read the cards to her.

Six o'clock came and it was time for the candlelight vigil. They opened the blinds and looked out at the crowd. The amount of people that were gathered together was incredible. The weather was a bit chilly, but it didn't matter because the love that exuded from the crowd produced warmth that you could feel. They cracked open the window just enough for the sound of the worship to fill Faith's room. It was a sound of love rising to heaven for a dear friend; a choral performance to God praising Him for His goodness and standing in faith that all would be well. They took pictures with their phones, so when Faith woke up, they would be able to show her this display of love.

Wednesday came and there was no change in Faith's condition, but they would not give up. They still took turns talking and telling stories, even laughing as they shared funny ones hoping something would cause a stirring in Faith. They watched for signs of movement, signs of reactions, even hoping they would see a twitch, but nothing happened. In and out they walked and paced trying to think of something that might reach her. They told her Thanksgiving was tomorrow and that they would still all be together; she would not be alone because they would not leave her. They played her favorite music and even sang along just like they would when they would be in the car driving around. Still no response, she lay lifeless.

The candlelight vigil was set to begin again, so they opened the window slightly and listened to the singing. Many people brought cards, so Sharon collected them and brought them up to the room after the vigil was over. The girls said they would read the cards to Faith tomorrow during the day.

Morning came, it was Thanksgiving Day and the whole gang was there. They brought in food so that none of them would have to leave at all that day. The group was hopeful, determined that Faith would recover. They continued talking to her; trying to get a reaction. The girls took turns reading the cards that people had brought the night before. The outpouring of love was indescribable. They stood around Faith's bed and laid their hands on her, praying that God would perform a miracle and heal her; they all believed He could and that He actually would.

Denise and Marcie decorated the room so it would be festive; they also hung up all the cards from everyone. The bulletin board in

Faith's room was covered in well wishes and pictures. Grandma told Denise that it made her think of a board she had seen downstairs the other day in the hospital lobby. Denise explained to Grandma that the board downstairs was for the person they refer to as "The Mustard Seed Angel". She told Grandma what was happening around the hospital and how the patients wanted to thank that person, but no one knew who it was. Grandma loved hearing the story, she smiled and said it was a lovely gesture; whoever thought about doing something that nice must be a very special person. The group agreed with her.

Time was moving right along; the group played some games and acted as if Faith was on one of the teams. They would joke and say, "Come on Faith, speak up, we know you got something to say." They were trying anything to get a rise out of her.

Marcie glanced at her watch and said, "The candlelight vigil is going to start in about ten minutes."

Danny looked outside and said, "You guys have to come and look at this!"

The group went to the window to see what he was talking about and to their surprise, they couldn't even see a speck of lawn. There were so many people out there holding up signs and getting ready for the vigil that it was like a sea of people.

"Faith I wish you could see this," said Denise, as she took out her phone and started taking pictures.

Grandma started to choke up at the display of love for her granddaughter. She walked over to the bedside and started to run her fingers through Faith's hair. "You are truly loved little one," said Grandma.

The friends took turns reading the signs out loud hoping that Faith could hear them. There was still no movement from Faith. The singing started, so they once again cracked open the window just slightly so the sound of praises would fill the room. The presence of God was undeniably strong. They gathered around Faith's bed singing, praying, and talking. Grandma reached down and adjusted the locket that was hanging on Faith's neck. Everyone remembered that it was the locket her parents had given to her at graduation. With her eyes welling up with tears, Denise asked Grandma if she knew what was in the locket.

"I have no idea," replied Grandma. "Faith's parents gave it to her empty and told her she would know what to put in it; that it would be something close to her heart. I'm assuming it contains pictures of her parents but, I don't really know."

The singing was still going on and God's presence was getting stronger and stronger.

"You know what," said Grandma. "Let's open it up and find out what's inside." Her hands were trembling as she gently lifted the locket just enough to grip it between her fingers. The room was so still, everyone holding their breath waiting to see what it contained. All of a sudden it was opened…mustard seeds spilled out all over Faith's chest and onto the bed. The group gasped as they realized Faith was "The Mustard Seed Angel." In that moment Faith's eyes opened. Tears streamed down their faces as they witnessed the miracle they were praying for. Danny ran to the window and screamed; "She's awake, she's awake, Faith is awake!!!" The crowd outside erupted with praise.

Faith's Locket

Epilogue

Although this is a fictitious story about the Braydan family and events that took place in their lives, the message within its words is truth. All of us will go through many things in this span of time we call life, things we understand and things we don't. Some events will be good, and some will be bad. What matters is how we live, how we persevere in all situations, how we help others, and the legacy we leave behind. God is a good God, the only true God; the Father, the Son, and the Holy Ghost and He will not leave us nor forsake us. He is always there, helping us through all things, even when we think He isn't. Hold on to Him and trust in Him even when you think you can't because He will never fail you.

If you don't know Jesus Christ as your personal Savior but you would like to, just say this prayer with me:

Lord, I come before you, a sinner in need of a Savior. I ask you to forgive me of my sins. I ask you to come into my heart and abide in me and I in you. I believe you are the one and only true begotten Son of God. I believe you died on the cross for the remission of my sins. I believe in three days you rose from the dead and you provide us with everlasting life. I give my life to you. I accept you as my Lord and Savior. In Jesus' name I pray.

If you've said this prayer let me know so I may offer praises to God for your Salvation. Welcome to the family of God.

Blessings,
Karen

FaithbooksbyKay@gmail.com

ACKNOWLEGEMENTS

Danny, you were hand-picked by God for me and I'll love you forever. You are my best friend, my Love, and I'm blessed to say my husband. God knew exactly what I needed when He created you. Thank you for believing in me and encouraging me to write this book. Thank you for the many hours spent on computer work and design. I couldn't have done this project without you. I love you babe.

Danny II, our first-born son, I love you with all my heart. I'm so thankful that God blessed us with you. Who knew a heart could love to this extent. Wow, what a gift! I am and always will be so proud of you. I love you D.

Brandon, our second son, you may have been born second, but I love you just the same. It's amazing how love works. God blessed us with the perfect addition to our family when he blessed us with you. I am and always will be so proud of you as well. I love you B.

The best accomplishment in my life is definitely being Mom to you two boys. My heart is overjoyed and thankful. I am blessed!!!!

Nicole, welcome to the family. You may not be daughter by birth, but you are in heart. I'm so thankful that God brought Brandon and you together as husband and wife. I'm also very proud of you. I love you BG.

Jasper, our first grandson. I love you so much. I'm so grateful that God blessed us with such a wonderful grandson. I live amazed at God's goodness. I'm very thankful for the special times we get to spend together. Gamma is so proud of you. I'll love you Forever, and ever, and ever, and ever…

Declan, our second grandson. I love you so much already too. I'm very happy and excited to have another grandson to love and spend special times with. What a blessing! God is so amazing! Gamma is so proud of you as well. I'll love you Forever, and ever, and ever, and ever…

Mom and Dad, I love you so much. Thank you for all you've done and for loving me! You taught me many valuable lessons and most of all you instilled love and respect into my life, which I am forever grateful. You raised me to Love God which is the best thing you could have done for me and I thank you with my whole heart. (We miss you Dad. Gone from our presence but not forgotten. You live on in our hearts.) I love you both.

Mom and Dad (in law), I couldn't have picked better in laws. We shared a lot of great times together and I am forever thankful. (We miss you Dad, but you live on in our hearts.) I love you both.

Marcie, thank you for all the work you did in the editing process. You have no idea how much it means to me. I'm blessed to have such a great friend. Thanks for the encouraging and kind words. I love you.

Denise, thank you for all the support you've always given me and for the encouraging words. I'm very blessed to have such a great friend. I love you.

To the rest of my family and friends…I thank God for you all. My life would not be the same without you in it.

You are all forever in my heart. My greatest blessings!!!

Love you now, forever, and always.

Karen

Made in the USA
Columbia, SC
12 March 2021